"Poignant and nasty as hell, Nat Cassidy's REST STOP is a thoughtful and sharply written chamber drama that veers off the rails into a profoundly devastating cosmic splatter spectacle."

—**Eric LaRocca**, author of
Things Have Gotten Worse Since We Last Spoke

"Somewhere between Saw and Sartre, there's a detour. Nat Cassidy's REST STOP is that roadside attraction, a funny, beautiful, and scary novella that leavens its introspection with blood-spatter and a dusting of spider legs. It's great!"

—**Adam Cesare**, author of
Clown in a Cornfield and *Influencer*

"REST STOP is an absurdist carnival, a suffocating funhouse filled with the watching eyes of nightmares and generational trauma that is equal parts gritty and witty. A fast-paced tale that wraps together hallucinatory, adrenaline-driven survival and endurance, illuminating the bloodiness of creation, and reflecting, quite literally, the desperation and struggle of humanity."

—**Ai Jiang**, Nebula and Bram Stoker
award-winning author of *Linghun*

"A gleefully vicious and relentless romp, REST STOP is Nat Cassidy at his most unhinged. Seriously, I'm scared of him now. This isn't a blurb, it's a restraining order."

—**Brian McAuley**, author of
Candy Cain Kills and *Curse of the Reaper*

"A little bit Stephen King's *1408*, a little bit Roger Corman visceral splatter, Cassidy's REST STOP is a locked room nightmare that spirals into mania, giving the reader exactly what they have come to expect from Cassidy's work."

—**C.S. Humble**, author of
That Light Sublime Trilogy

"Nat Cassidy's REST STOP is a lean, mean, and claustrophobic fever dream of blood and venom. It's everything you're afraid of (and oh so much more) when you pull into a lonely gas station in the middle of the night. As sharp as broken glass, this blood-soaked novella is equal parts slasher and self-realization. With keen insight into the pains of overtaking our former selves, and how much it can hurt to become someone better, Cassidy keeps the pedal to the metal in a unbearably tense story that rushes headlong into the unexpected. REST STOP is a punk rock guitar solo—fast, brutal, and melodic—and Cassidy is the one shredding his fingers on the strings. One of my favorite reads of the year."

—**Tyler Jones**, author of
Burn the Plans and *Heavy Oceans*

"A delightfully gory, witty, and terrifying rollercoaster ride that left me literally gasping—and also a poignantly affecting story of familial trauma and existential despair that creeps under your skin and stays there. From start to finish, Rest Stop hits every skillfully arranged note."

—**Sunny Moraine**, author of
Your Shadow Half Remains

REST STOP

A NOVELLA

NAT CASSIDY

SHORTWAVE
PUBLISHING

Cover design and interior layout by Alan Lastufka.

First Edition published October 2024.

10 9 8 7 6 5 4 3 2 1

ISBN 978-1-959565-36-9 (Paperback)
ISBN 978-1-959565-37-6 (eBook)

To all our grandparents.

Heads up: this story contains a lot of bug stuff, snake stuff, face trauma, religious trauma, antisemitism, claustrophobia, general existential angst, and a little suicidal ideation. It also might get some yacht rock stuck in your head, but no need to thank me for that.

THE BIG BANG; LET THERE BE YACHT ROCK; BROKEN HEARTS; MOTHERFUCKING SNOBALLS

All is either darkness or chaos.

The deep space obscurity of midnight or the careless incoherence of lights and colors speeding past, expanding, tumbling, destined only to wink out in the rearview. Barely any form, let alone any meaning.

Until—

Splat!

A bug the size of an adult human thumb collides with his windshield, presenting its insides in a wet bouquet across the glass.

"Sweet Jesus!" Abe exclaims.

"What?" His older brother's worried voice, coming from the phone plugged into the dashboard. "What happened?"

"Nothing. Just a huge fucking dragonfly or something. Christ. Thing was big enough to have a social security number."

"Well, it's summer," his brother says, always helpful.

"Yeah. Thanks."

Abe engages the wipers. The remnants of the bug smear across the windshield in stubborn, arcing streaks. He tries adding a little windshield fluid. The bug refuses to be forgotten.

For the briefest of moments, Abe feels a touch of something like dread at the base of his spine, though he has no idea why.

"Look," he tells his brother, "can I get back to concentrating on what I'm doing? Or do you need to tell me another thirty times how I should've started driving sooner?"

"Hey, you're the one who decided to still be on the road at," a pause while his brother looks at a clock somewhere, "one forty-five a.m. I tried to get you to leave earlier."

"I'm also the one who explained I have a gig in a few days and we had to cram a rehearsal in since I'm being dragged to somebody's hospital bedside for the foreseeable future."

"It wasn't Bobbe's idea to have a stroke before your big gig, Abe."

"It's not a 'big gig,' okay, it's just a 'gig.' But thanks for the condescension."

"Fine."

"And if anyone would purposefully time a stroke to fuck with my life, it's Bobbe."

His brother declines to respond. He's exhausted too; Abe can hear it.

"I'm hanging up now," Abe says at last. "The road is starting to look like the end of *2001*, so I gotta focus."

"Please be safe. We don't need you to die too."

"Bobbe would be furious about being upstaged. If she *does* die, which I still don't think is possible."

"The doctors said—"

"I know."

"And mom really wants you here before that—"

"I *know*. Can I please hang up now?"

"Lemme know when you're like an hour away. You sure you're okay to drive? You have me worried now."

"Yes. Unless I purposefully drive myself off a cliff."

"Abe."

"I'm fine!"

"Fine. Just, one last thing—"

"What? Jesus!"

"*That.* Can you cool it with the Jesuses and the Christs? You know how much she hates that. I don't know if she can hear anything right now, but. . ."

Abe chuckles. "Hey. Maybe it'll make her mad enough to snap out of her coma."

"Ha. Maybe. She'll wake up to yell at you for being a bad Jew."

"She'll hop out of bed to write me out of the will, like she did to Uncle Mike for being rude to her at that dinner once."

"And his kids too. Don't forget she wrote his kids out. Just 'cause he asked her to stop being racist to the waiter."

"Hey, what if she wakes up and the stroke has made her an actually pleasant person?"

"That'd be a miracle."

"I just might start believing in God then."

The brothers fall into brief, guilt-tinged giggles, thinking of their own emotional infarctions with their not-so-beloved grandmother: Bobbe Meydl, their mother's mother, the only grandparent they've ever known.

Then they remember they're grownups, not little kids sharing a bedroom. They repeat their goodbyes and disconnect, leaving Abe alone in silence.

It was a long enough call that the playlist Abe had been blasting doesn't automatically come back on, so for the moment, all he has is the sound of his wheels barreling over the mostly empty highway to underscore his thoughts.

So many thoughts.

He considers turning on the radio, or maybe listening to a podcast. He doesn't do that, though—because it's August, deep in the cursed year of 2016, and all anyone can talk about now is the upcoming election. The blonde, bloviating businessman versus the blonde, cackling e-mail lady. Abe takes a little comfort that E-mail Lady's all but guaranteed to win, but still. What a shitshow. As if this year hasn't been traumatic enough. Bowie dead. Prince dead. George Martin dead. Alan Rickman dead. Chyna dead. Abe fuckin' Vigoda dead.

And, of course, Abe's own troubles. His *tsuris*, as Bobbe would call them, no doubt in her sneering, mocking way.

"Splat," he whispers, almost like an invocation. It's hard not to stare at the base reduction left on the glass.

He pulls up the playlist he'd been listening to earlier. Stabs 'Play' with a vengeance.

The next song begins. The Doobie Brothers. "What a Fool Believes."

During the day, Abe, who is the bassist/vocalist for a death-metal-math-rock duo called Darwin's Foëtus, hates—despises—*loathes*—shit like the Doobie Brothers. But alone in his car? Barreling down the open throat of midnight on a barely peopled highway in the middle of the country for a trip he desperately does not want to be taking? There's only one proper response any mortal being can have to the smooth vocal stylings of Mr. Michael McDonald.

"FUCK YESSSSS!" Abe punches the steering wheel in celebration and starts scream-singing along. As with all Michael McDonald songs, he only really knows the vowel sounds, but that doesn't matter.

What matters is he's looking past the bug guts to the dark road beyond.

ХХХ

He'd lied to his brother. There'd been no last-minute rehearsal. The main reason Abe hadn't left the house until the last possible moment was because he frankly just didn't want to. So he'd puttered around his apartment, finding things to take his attention. A sock drawer that needed to be culled of socks with holes in them. A refrigerator that needed emptying. A beloved Ibanez BTB745 that needed new strings. He would've kept finding important tasks like that forever if his brother hadn't called to ask how the trip was going.

In fact, Abe's bandmate Ty had *begged* Abe to rehearse, but Abe ducked Ty's phone calls and texts, as he'd been doing for the past couple weeks. The only time they'd spoken since setting the gig up had been when Abe let him know he had to go out of town yesterday.

That had freaked Ty out. He started whining, pleading—just a quick rehearsal, please, just to make sure we're on top of our shit.

Abe assured him he'd be back in time for the show, and then left him on read. Was, in fact, enjoying making Ty twist in the wind a little.

Ty is always annoying before a show, even under normal circumstances. He likes to pretend like each and every performance is that scene in the movie where the record exec sneaks into the back of the club and is so blown away by the talent onstage that a major label contract is offered on the spot. Abe doesn't think record execs are even a thing anymore.

But Abe knows why Ty is so concerned about this particular gig.

He'd say it's because of their *previous* gig at Club Congress. That disaster. He'd say it's because they need to prove themselves—to the venue and to each other, that their band is worth saving.

But Abe knows what's really on Ty's mind.

The Doobie Brothers are fading out now. He stops his scream-singing, says her name to his empty car with a mourner's sigh.

"Jenna."

Two soft syllables that slice like razor wire.

Oh, Jenna.

Beautiful, quixotic, intelligent-eyed Jenna.

Smart, funny, passionate Jenna. Awesome fashion-sensed Jenna. Who always cheers loudly for their songs even when no one else is in the crowd, and who's never afraid to call you on your bullshit when your lyrics are clichéd or problematic.

Darwin's Foëtus's next gig is going to be Jenna and Ty's first "official" gig as a couple. *That's* what Ty really cares about. Impressing his new girlfriend. Making her proud. Making her want to be scooped up in his arms afterwards, so they can sneak away somewhere to celebrate and proba-bly—

"Fuck," Abe exhales, horrified to feel an actual tear leaking out of his eye. He wipes it away, embarrassed and furious. Christ, he has it bad for this girl.

Don't call me a 'girl,' he imagines Jenna saying. *I'm thirty-one years old. Also, watch it with the C-word, remember?*

The next song on his yacht rock playlist begins. "Summer Breeze," Seals and Croft. Abe turns the music up to try to drown out his thoughts.

Two a.m. on the dot now; precisely the number of cars that are sharing the highway with him.

Out of the deep-sea darkness, a billboard floats past. Wavy, kitschy letters proclaiming:

TRUMBULL FARMS
SNAKE AND SPIDER HOUSE
Visit . . . If You Dare
NEXT EXIT

Flanking the lettering are a few photos of—surprise, surprise—snakes and spiders. Truth in advertising. Always nice to see.

That'd be a cool spot to visit during the day. Maybe on the drive back. Kill a little more time before showing up and relieving Ty's anxieties. Plus, it'd be nice to visit some of nature's more pleasant creatures after being around his grandmother.

Thinking of creepy crawlies, his gaze is drawn to the guts on the windshield again.

Oh, Jenna. I'm the bug. You're the windshield.

He wants to roll his eyes at the sentiment, but he refrains. The movement might cause more tears to spill out.

What about Bobbe? What's she in this metaphor?

"The darkness," he mutters, and gives a wet chuckle.

Even stupid, piece of shit Ty knows how Abe feels about his grandmother. One rehearsal, Ty had been reminiscing about his own perfect and cherished Nana, who baked cookies and sent birthday cards with a ten-dollar bill tucked inside, even into adulthood.

Abe had scoffed. "That's wild. My grandmother's one of the worst people I've ever met."

"Your *grandmother*?" As if grandmothers were some trusted brand. "Seriously?"

"Seriously." Abe started fiddling around on his bass. Minor key riffs and runs. "For just a taste: she tells me I'm a failure *every* time I see her. Those are her exact words. 'Abraham, are you still wasting your life?' That's how she says hello."

"Damn." Ty followed along on guitar.

"And let's see. . . . She chased my mom with a hammer once for dating a Black guy in the '70s. My mom ran away and lived in a park for a few weeks after that."

"Fuck!"

"Oh, and she's the *worst* whenever she meets any other immigrants. She'll start quizzing them on where they're from, and then start telling them how *she* had it worse as a child. That they should be glad they're not her—which I'm sure they are. I've seen her spit at people. I've seen her flip them off, to their face. She's rude. She's mean. And the only reason she's not constantly being beaten with sticks is because she's this tiny old lady."

"She sucks."

"She *really* sucks."

"Why is she like that?"

Abe shrugged. "The war? She grew up in this tiny village in Poland that got sandwiched between the Nazis and the Commies and—"

"Oh, man, did she get sent to a *camp?*" Ty whispered it, the way he did whenever he spoke of something serious. Like he expected to get in trouble. Beautiful, dumb Ty.

"Nah," Abe replied. "Some extended family did, but she got to stay with some family friends. I guess things didn't actually get bad for her until right *after* the war. I dunno. Trauma's trauma, but I think some people are still just born assholes."

Suddenly—*splat*—he finds himself wondering: what would *Jenna* be like as a grandmother?

Their whole impossible future flashes by in an instant. They have kids, grow old, watch their kids have kids. Jenna becomes one of those cool grandmas with tattoos and a record collection. She curses and makes naughty jokes and sips whiskey (but never too much). She has long, silver-blue hair—or maybe a wicked bob—and every time she looks at Abe she smiles a warm smile that says, *look how far we've come.* That says she's never once regretted her decision to fall in love with a man who, sure, doesn't look like your everyday romantic hero, but who has a heart of gold and fingers of—

"ABE!" He shouts at himself. "STOP IT!" He whips his head back and forth.

This is all way too depressing. Not even summer breezes blowing through jasmine can keep the midnight blues away. He's also getting hungry. And thirsty. More than that, he wants sugar. Lots and lots of sugar.

He should get gas, too—and maybe wipe off the bug guts from his windshield before the idea of driving off a cliff really *does* become tantalizing.

Just as he has that thought, a radiant green and white sign with the image of a gas pump emerges from the darkness.

"And the Lord said let there be a gas station, and it was so. See? Miracles do happen."

Mouth watering at the thought of Icees and beef jerky and, holy shit, some Hostess motherfucking SnoBalls, Abe glides smoothly onto the exit ramp.

PARIAHS; BIGGEST PARTS; UNPLEASANT FRIENDS

The parking lot isn't empty. Two other cars sit next to each other near the entrance to the gas station's convenience store. There's also a powder blue VW Westfalia that's as far away from those two cars as it can get while still being parked up at the front. It looks like some pariah animal at the local watering hole, not welcome to hang with the other gazelles or hippos.

Abe pulls into his own spot, then sits for a moment.

The song on his playlist has changed to "Biggest Part of Me," by Ambrosia.

Another legitimately good song Daytime Abe would never admit to liking, full of complex changes and interesting harmonies. It actually might make for a delightful (and safely ironic) cover. He can imagine singing it onstage, looking out into the crowd, making direct, unequivocal eye contact with Jenna. She'd probably laugh. Not a mocking laugh but a delighted one. A laugh that would settle into a warm, appreciative smile. It'd probably make her happy. It might make her blush.

It might even make her *think*.

He angrily turns off the engine, killing the song.

Snacks first, then gas and windshield cleaning. Let that bug have a few moments longer to be memorialized in this cruel, stupid universe.

He's reaching to unplug his phone from the dash when a text comes in. His brother, who apparently doesn't sleep. The message reads:

All still good? Updated ETA?

"Ugh! Leave me alone! Fuck *everybody!*" Abe snarls, flipping off the screen.

He quickly gets out, leaving his phone in the car.

XXX

As he sulkily trudges his way to the front door of the convenience store, he passes by the blue van. He's already started to anthropomorphize it—poor loner van, probably too awesome for the other cars to appreciate. *I feel you, Lonely Westfalia.*

A band he once knew called the Benson Ashe used to tour around in a green Westfalia, and that had always seemed like a fun time, so Abe gives this one an appraising look.

All its windows are curtained from the inside. Totally private. Probably means they do a lot of drugs in there. Rock on, Lonely Westfalia; live your truth.

Then he notices the license plate. A vanity plate. It takes him a moment to understand what it means, but as soon as he does a shudder ripples through him. Suddenly, not being able to see inside the van seems like a very bad thing.

"Jesus," he whispers.

We're not friends anymore, Lonely Westfalia.

He hurries over to the store, now desperate to get inside. This parking lot has gotten too dark and it feels like that van, with its impenetrable windows, is swelling in size, blotting out what little light there is.

When he reaches the front door, he turns back around, as if to double check what he just read.

The front license plate is the same.

CR8 H8

Create Hate.

APPLE PIE; SILENT SCREAM;
A QUICK BATHROOM
DETOUR BEFORE HITTING
THE ROAD

Safe inside the store—so bright, so blissfully cool after even just a few moments of the muggy summer air—and he feels better. Sometimes capitalism knows how to hold you just right.

Abe starts wandering up and down the aisles, idly scanning snacks, keeping his head down so as to not make eye contact with whatever psycho owns that van outside. Soon enough, he's lost in his snack options and his thoughts.

Maybe it's because she's dying, but Abe's been thinking of his grandmother a lot lately. Thinking *as* his grandmother. Her accented, sneery voice randomly buzzsaws into his brain, offering all sorts of unwelcome, unhelpful commentary. As he starts grabbing brightly colored treats off of the well-stocked shelves, here she comes again.

No wonder this country is so fat and lazy. Look at all the poison they stuff into their faces. Disgusting.

Abe shakes his head, not just at the sentiment (*fuck you, Grannie, this food is dope*), but at the implication. Because whenever she said something disparaging about "this country," it carried the implication that *Abe* was among the fat and lazy too. That, in fact, Abe was an avatar of horrid Americanness. *That's me. Abraham Yehuda Neer, right up there with baseball and apple pie.*

He supposes he *gets* it. To an extent. Meydl always looked at Abe and, to a lesser extent, his brother, as not just creatures from another planet but as betrayers of their true faith and culture. After everything she and her family went through, it makes sense she'd be a little sensitive about stuff like that. But it's called assimilation, Grandma. It doesn't have to be a *bad* thing. Hell, their ancestors might've done well to do a little bit more of that over the millennia—maybe then they wouldn't have been such a frequent target.

And it's not like Abe doesn't want to be Jewish. There's a lot he digs about the religion, the history. Contrary to what he joked to his brother earlier, he's not necessarily against the idea of the existence of God, either—or at least a God-like *Energy* out there. It's the arbitrary rituals he doesn't care about. Being Jewish is cool and all, but who in their right mind ever volunteers for extra homework? Who doesn't love the occasional pork chop or cheeseburger?

Sometimes he wonders if maybe Bobbe's unpleasantness isn't actually more generational than religious. He has another friend, a metal bassist named Win, who's half-Korean and has a similar relationship with his grandmother. Win's *halmoni* lived through her own horrors during the war, courtesy of the Japanese, and Win thought the things she witnessed were a big reason why she'd never been, let's say, interested in social niceties. "But, I mean, that entire generation's gotta be *so* messed up, right?" Win said over post-show beers once. "That's the thing about a world war. Everyone that age, no matter where they're from, went through things we can't imagine. Things *we'll* never go through. At least, I hope not."

Abe supposes that might be true. On the other hand, hadn't he met plenty of nice old people with faint numbers tattooed on their forearms when he was a kid? People who radiated a love of life? Why should Bobbe's travails give her license to be such a shit all the time? Why should anybody's? We're all in this mess together. Things like religion, like nationalities, are just trivia. We're all just bugs against the windshield of time, right?

As if looking for an amen, he finally glances up at the other customers in the store and his thoughts cut off abruptly, like somebody screamed in his ear.

No one screamed.

Quite the opposite. Except for the crinkle of the bag of Corn Nuts in his hand, this place is silent as a tomb.

Because there *are* no other customers.

The store is completely empty. Abe's been so wrapped up in his thoughts, it hadn't registered until just this moment.

"The hell?" he mutters.

The Icee machines whir. The refrigerators hum. And yet. . . not a soul around to operate or browse through any of it. Not even someone at the counter.

Weird. Especially considering the three cars in the lot. Where could everyone be?

"Uhhh. . ." He gives a stupid, disbelieving laugh.

He goes to the front door. Looks out into the night. The cars are still there. That van—

(*create hate*)

—is practically leering at him.

For the first time in his life, he actively wills the voice of his grandmother to come back into his head. Keep him company. Chide him for being silly.

She's totally silent too. Of course she is. When has she ever done anything helpful?

He turns back to face the store. Scan it from this angle. Still no signs of anybody. Next to him, the newspaper stands blare headlines and photos about, what else, the election. Both candidates, frozen in mid-roar. Here in this gas station, even *they're* rendered mute.

"Okayyyyy..." He tries to shake off the unease, get back to his supply-gathering. Any second now, a clerk will emerge from the backroom and make things feel normal again.

As he reaches the beverage section, something catches his attention. Something on the floor.

He bends down to get a better look.

It's a small, plastic googly eye. The kind a kid might glue onto a craft project and then shake it so the pupil rolls around.

Huh.

Much like the smeared guts of the insect against his windshield, for some reason this little plastic circle fills him with a heavy, unspeakable dread.

I think I wanna get the fuck outta here.

"Yeah," he mutters. "Good idea."

Except, he really should pee. He has hours and hours left of his drive and, if this stop is spooking him so badly, he should maybe avoid stopping at any other middle-of-nowhere gas stations before the sun comes up. Don't look a gift toilet in the mouth now.

Fine. Peeing will be his final attempt at buying time. If he comes out of the bathroom and the place is still empty, he'll grab his snacks, leave a ten-dollar bill on the counter, and make tracks. And if he just so happens to grab more than ten dollars' worth? Well, you shoulda been better at your job, Check Out Guy.

He crosses over to what's clearly the bathroom: a plain white door on the opposite wall, in between a beverage case and a display of shirts and hats and a couple ice scrapers.

There's a sheet of printer paper taped to the door:

No Key.
If It's Locked, It's OCCUPADO

Under which someone had handwritten:

*THAT MEANS
"SOMEONE'S POOPING"
IN FRENCH*

Great. Buncha comedians run this joint.

He puts his hand on the knob, then stops. What if everyone's hiding in there right now? What if he walks in on an orgy-in-progress, three cars' worth of naked weirdos, holding their breaths and their naughty bits, waiting for Abe to leave so they can resume their midnight game of Fill 'er Up? What if the Create Hate guy is their fuck maestro and this is how he goes about cr8ing?

What if they ask him to join?

Best excuse I'd have yet to keep Bobbe waiting, I guess.

He turns the knob and pushes the door open.

A completely empty and unremarkable bathroom stands before him. Just a single toilet sorta deal; not even a stall to hide behind. Not occupado. No one pooping in French.

Abe sighs, maybe in relief, maybe in disappointment, and steps inside.

THE POINT OF THE JOKE

The dread recedes a little but doesn't disappear. The sound of his peeing feels too loud, too exposed, so he starts humming the first yacht rock song that pops in his head while he finishes up.

At least his body feels a little relief.

Peeing is the best. Whoever invented peeing was a stand-up guy, hyuck hyuck.

When he's done, he steps to the sink to rinse off his hands. Studies his face in the mirror. An all-too-familiar thought:

This is not the face of the guy who Gets the Girl.

Gets her to laugh, maybe. Gets her a thoughtful present for her birthday, maybe. But outside a Woody Allen or Adam Sandler movie, where the point of the joke is that the nebbish somehow has sex appeal, no one's throwing themselves at someone like Abe's feet. With his wavy, thick hair that covers his head fully but doesn't *do* anything interesting. With his skin, still faintly marked from a merciless bout of teenage acne. With his somehow simultaneously pudgy and scrawny frame. With his prominent, oh-so-semitic nose, which one particularly nasty bully in middle school had dubbed his "Jew Beak." *That* had prompted Abe's first—and, up until a few weeks ago, his only—fight.

Hell, Abe barely even looks the part as a *musician*. He'll never forget that one gig where the club owner asked him, "So, you're the band's manager, right?" That's when Abe had decided to grow his hair out, no matter how awkward it looked.

Despondency over his severely dented heart replaces his dread for the moment. He stares at his stupid, shmuck face in the spotty, streaky glass of the gas station bathroom. Examines every angle.

It's time to admit it. Jenna and Ty make sense. Jenna can have her pick of literally any human she wants, and Ty is a big, handsome, Übermensch rockstar with a jaw that doesn't quit and a golden retriever sweetness. Abe can play the bassline of a death metal song in 9/8 time while screaming lyrics on top of it, and he's pretty good at *Super Smash Brothers*, but he doesn't have much else to recommend himself. Besides, what was that old Groucho Marx quote? "I wouldn't want to belong to any club that had me as a member?" Something like that.

Just like that, he decides he's just going to be happy for Jenna and Ty. Hey: if Ty and Jenna make it work, at least Jenna will be around more. She'll come to more rehearsals, more gigs, more afterparties. She can tell more of her corny jokes in her dry, wicked monotone. She can show Abe more panels of her sci-fi graphic novel-in-progress. They can get into more arguments about movies and books. Just friends, but still: friends.

That's right, Bobbe Meydl says. *Be happy for them. She's not one of us anyway, Abraham. Stick to your own kind.*

"Yeah," he grumbles. "What I really want is someone who'll turn into you in a few decades, Bobbe. That's some hot shit."

Okay, so maybe he's a little bitter. Know what the best cure for bitterness is, though?

"I'm gonna get me an Icee *and* a Doctor Pepper *and* some SnoBalls *and* some goddamn motherfuckin' Fruit Stripe gum if they have it," he tells his reflection. Mirror Abe gives a resolute nod.

He dries his hands on his pants and is planning the exact combo of flavors he's going to dump into a single Icee cup when he bounces off the door and stumbles backwards into the room.

"The fuck?"

He tries the door again.

It won't open.

The handle goes down, popping out the handle lock he'd depressed when he'd entered the bathroom, but when he pushes on the door, it sticks fast in its frame.

Is he not pushing the handle down far enough? He puts his shoulder into it.

Still no luck.

Has he somehow... locked himself inside? He's done a lot of clumsy, stupid shit in his life, but this would be pretty impressive. How would it even be possible? The only lock he can see is on the handle and he'd heard it diseng—

There are four holes a few inches above the handle. The faint outline of a box around them. A smaller, equally faint outline across the seam of the door. Like a deadbolt had once been there, and...

...and what? Moved? To the other side of the door?

"The fuck," he says again. Quieter, but no less baffled.

He presses on the door. It *does* feel like something at approximately that height on the other side was holding the door shut. Perhaps he'd been too busy reading the dumb jokes on that stupid sign to notice there'd been a deadbolt on the outside of the door?

Maybe. But the thing about deadbolts is they don't engage automatically. Someone's gotta slide them in place. And that deadbolt obviously had to have been pulled back when he'd opened the door in the first place. Which means. . .

A sick, churning feeling in his guts. His heart begins to pound.

"Hello?" He shouts into the door. "*Hello?*" Then, stupidly: "Someone's in here!"

He continues to shake the handle. Surely, this has gotta be a mistake. Someone cleaning up for the night didn't think to check if the room was occupado first. Or maybe a little kid wandered over and slid the lock shut while his mom was grabbing some late-night snacks? Maybe that's where that weird fucking googly eye came from?

Doesn't seem likely. Then again, neither does a bathroom door with a deadbolt on the wrong side.

Finally, he stops. Catches his breath. Tries not to let panic surge too high inside his chest.

Pressing an ear to the metal, he listens carefully for any noise on the other side.

The empty gas station convenience store—which he now knows *can't* be empty—offers nothing in return.

FEARLESS; WRITING ON
THE WALL; NOISES IN
THE CEILING

A few more pounds on the door. A few more shouts.

"*Helloooo?* Is anyone out there? This friggin' door is locked or something! This isn't funny!"

He presses all over the door, as if there might be some sort of secret panel. Nothing.

Finally, with a great roll of his eyes, he leans his forehead against the metal surface, weakly whacking the door with the bottom of his fist.

"Come onnnnnnnn."

When his energy peters out, he peels himself away and begins pacing the room, taking stock of what's in here with him.

A toilet.

A thin plastic brush and a plunger with a moderately thick wooden dowel.

A sink. A soap dispenser. A mirror (Mirror Abe gives a sympathetic head shake: you believe this shit?).

There's also a vent in the ceiling towards the center of the room. The vent hangs down a little from its aperture. Maybe he can grab onto that and pull his way out through the ceiling? He files that thought away as a Worst-Case Scenario sort of idea.

Other than that, there's not much of note beyond a few random phrases scribbled onto the wall, mostly clustered by the toilet paper holder. Prime real estate for bored squatters. "Be fearless — fart as loud as your anus allows" and "THINGS I HATE: 1. GRAFFITI 2. LISTS 3. IRONY" and "TRUMP 2016 MAGA," under which someone else had scrawled "I just shit out a better president."

There's also one sentence written on the wall opposite the mirror. Abe reads it carefully, in case it's somehow a clue.

SALLY SPARROW DUCK NOW

"Awesome," he sighs. No idea what that means, but he's pretty sure there are no indications anyone else has suffered his particular problem in this room before.

Time to get drastic, then. Time to kick the fucker down.

He stands in front of the door, sizing it up like a boxer trying to intimidate his opponent. Abe hasn't been to the gym in a minute and leg flexibility isn't one of his key selling points as a bassist. There's also nothing to really hold onto for balance, so he's just going to have to try to hammer kick this bitch from a freestanding position.

"Piece of cake," he huffs, already out of breath at the thought of it. Maybe he'll get one less sugary treat once he gets out of this mess.

"Fuck that. When I get outta here, I'm eating every Twinkie in the place." He swings his leg up and out, hitting the door with all his might.

It shakes in its frame but, overall, seems pretty unimpressed with his efforts.

He kicks again.

He kicks a third time, as hard as he can—so hard he almost loses his balance and goes careening backwards, just barely managing to stay upright and not Crocodile Mile his way into the piss pool on the floor.

The door remains unmoved. Either Abe is weaker than he likes to imagine, or the deadbolt on the other side of the door is screwed in mercilessly tight.

Okay. Kicking isn't going to work. Neither, he learns a few moments later, is ramming his shoulder against the door. All he gets is an ache along that side of his body, and some hot, private embarrassment for his troubles. That deadbolt must be pretty heavy-duty.

Now what? Just wait for rescue? Chalk this up to bad luck and/or being careful what you wish for when he wished for an excuse to be late to his destination?

A noise. Barely audible. A low *rumblethunk* in the ceiling.

His mouth goes dry.

"Hello?" He clears his throat. "*Hello?*"

Another thump. The air conditioning coming on?

Yeah, that must be it. Just the air conditioning.

Definitely not the sound of someone crawling through the ceiling towards him.

Definitely not the soft titter of someone giggling.

Abe has a couple seconds where he's able to convince himself he's just being paranoid.

Then the biggest spider he's ever seen falls, as if pushed, out of the vent and drops to the floor.

BORIS

A prank.

Some plastic gag toy. Has to be.

No way are there real spiders *that* big. The size of his actual hand.

The fake spider lays where it fell. Immobile. Inanimate. Which makes sense because the only other times Abe has seen a spider like this are for Halloween decorations, and thankfully, Halloween decorations aren't—

The spider scrambles towards the wall. Very fucking alive. Very fucking real.

Abe goes rigid. He'd piss his pants if he hadn't already gone.

"Is. . . somebody up there?" Abe asks the ceiling in a high, tremulous voice. Gentle. Almost absurdly soft. Not wanting to agitate his new companion. He listens hard for any movement above. The ceiling is low, maybe eight feet? Seven and a half? Abe could scrape it with his fingertips if he jumps, and the thought of someone crouched so close to the top of his head, quiet, listening, lurking, is beyond unsettling.

Regardless, there's no response.

Back to the spider. It's given up trying to crawl up the wall. Now it's tucking itself into the corner, hopefully as scared as Abe is. Even from this distance, he can't help but marvel how hairy and angular the thing is. Like a spider cobbled together with discarded rat parts.

"Uhhhh, so where'd *you* come from?" Abe asks, putting on his best chill, go-along-to-get-along demeanor. He doesn't know if spiders appreciate such things. "You, uh. . . from around here?"

A sign flashes in Abe's memory. Trumbull Farms.

"An escaped convict, maybe?"

The spider only glares at him. Abe can feel the multiple eyes sizing him up, breaking him down.

"You're a tarantula, right? You look scary but you're pretty docile? You've just got a bad reputation? I can dig that."

If Abe ever had occasion to visit Trumbull Farms, he would have seen this particular specimen on display—not a tarantula, but a Sydney funnel-web spider. The signage would've informed him that the Sydney funnel-web spider isn't deadly. Not usually, at least. But it *is* "a favorite here at the Farm, because, as you see, they're not shy! In fact, they're very aggressive. And those fangs can bite down hard enough to break a mouse's skull!"

Now Abe raises his voice, again trying to reach the (maybe? possibly?) person in the ceiling. He feels like a supplicant, begging some remote, inimical deity.

"Hey, this is really funny. Super funny bit. I dig it." He listens for a moment. "Is this being filmed?" Another long pause. "Maybe I can help you out? I did theater in high school? And I did improv for a couple semesters in college? I could. . . y'know, help you out with bits and. . . stuff?"

The presence in the ceiling—if there is one—stays silent.

Meanwhile, the spider raises two of its front legs. It makes Abe think of a magician preparing onlookers for a feat of wizardry. He doesn't like it one bit.

"Look, little guy," Abe gulps. "I don't want to hurt you. And I'm like four hundred times your size, so I probably *could* hurt you. So, just stay over there, okay? We're just gonna be super chill roommates until someone comes and lets us out. Cool?"

The spider's other legs ripple; each one briefly lifting off the ground, testing its readiness.

"I'm just gonna go. . . over here." Abe backs towards the opposite wall, pressing himself into the most diametric corner possible. "Super chill roomies. No stress. All good. Do you know The Who? John Entwhistle? One of the greatest bassists of all time? He's got a song called 'Boris the Spider.' Fucking dope song, it's—although, he. . . he kills the spider with a book at the end, never mind, you don't need to hear it, it's not very good. But the name's cool, right? Boris?"

The spider puts its legs down. It seems mollified.

"Yeah. Boris. We're cool, Boris. Best buds, me and Boris."

Meanwhile, Abe looks around for something to murder Boris with. Just in case.

Nothing reveals itself. Neither the toilet bowl brush nor plunger look serious enough to deliver a killing blow. He could maybe trap Boris under the upturned trash can. But probably he'll just have to resort to a good ole fashioned stomping—and for some reason stepping on something so big, so *complex*, as Boris the giant spider makes him wanna barf. He'll feel the exoskeleton break. He'll feel joints dislodge. He might have to do it multiple times.

Fuuuuck.

His grandmother pipes up. *Pathetic. Your goyishe friend with the chin would never be so afraid to kill a little spider. . .*

Before he can assure his imagined grandmother that he's not, in fact, afraid, Boris makes the first move.

"Whoa, whoa, what are we doing?" Abe tries to back further into his corner.

Boris has taken a few tentative steps forward, sticking close to the base of the wall. Now, a few more steps. And a few more. In no real hurry, which somehow makes it even worse, like watching the tide roll in while you're buried up to your neck on the beach. Abe decides maybe the toilet bowl brush or the plunger don't seem so useless after all. He circles around the room opposite Boris, a slow-motion pursuit.

Of course, both the brush and the plunger are tucked behind the toilet, so when he finally reaches his destination, Abe has to turn his back on Boris to pick his weapon. He opts for the plunger, which then gets tangled up with the brush. He has to jimmy it out of its place for a precious second or two.

When he turns back around, Boris is gone.

The wall that Boris had been skimming against is empty. All the walls of the small square room, in fact.

"Fuck. Where'd you go, Boris? Fuck! Where'd you g—"

The huge spider is already at his feet. Rearing back. Lifting its massive fangs, which Abe can see with horrible clarity.

Boris means business.

"NOPE!" Abe tries to do several things at once. He tries to swat Boris with the plunger. He tries to kick Boris with his shoe. He tries to run away.

What he manages to do is flick the top of Boris with the plastic end of the weapon in his hand and also take a half step to the side with his right foot. His foot meets the puddle on the floor and then, in apocalyptic slow motion, Abe loses his balance and falls onto the tile.

The graze with the plunger knocked Boris back a few inches and stunned the spider momentarily. But now Abe is laid out before him and Boris isn't going to miss the opportunity.

The spider rears up again. It's grown somehow—at least the size of a small dog and its fangs are long, black daggers jutting from two thick extensions that look like a child's drawing of bodybuilder biceps.

Those fangs come straight for Abe's face.

Then, somehow, the next thing Abe knows: Boris is flattened against the floor and the heel of his left hand is radiating with ice-white numbness.

Abe scrambles away, at first just relieved Boris doesn't pursue. He starts to put together what happened. He'd swung his free fist down onto Boris's back before Boris could strike. He'd done it out of pure panic, so hard and frantic that some of Boris's guts had shot out of his spinnerets.

Even though the thought of touching that hairy carapace still fills him with panic-barbed nausea, Abe reaches forward, picks up the still-twitching spider, and hurls it with all his might against the wall. As his hand grips Boris's body, Abe thinks, *this doesn't feel right, my hand doesn't feel right,* but his thirst for vengeance is stronger. Boris the Spider, the would-be face-biter, now lays upside down, legs curled, against the wall, fully shrunken to the size of an impressive—but *real*—spider.

Abe staggers to his feet, breathing hard. The kind of breathing that brings with it low, gravelly vocalizations. Eventually he gathers enough grunts to form a sentence.

"Fuck you, Boris! Never liked that song anyway."

He stares at the spider for about five full minutes.

His hand won't stop throbbing. His pinky and ring finger aren't curling the way they should. But at least the crisis is over.

Hoping some cold water will numb the pain a little, he heads over to the sink, and that's when he remembers where Boris came from.

"You fucking enjoying this, asshole?" He calls over his shoulder to the ceiling, running his hand under the tap. The water helps—but only a little. "Having fun? You *dick*? Super hilarious prank! I think I've got piss all over me. And I have a gig in a few days and I might've just broken my fucking h—"

Movement catches his eye in the mirror. His words cut off.

He spins around, hoping that what he thinks he saw in the glass isn't what's actually coming out of the ceiling vent.

It is.

Oh God, it is.

And it's in this moment Abe realizes—perhaps belatedly—that none of this is a prank.

It's in this moment he realizes how fucked he truly is.

He begins to scream.

Louder than he's ever screamed in his soon-to-be-over life.

SEVEN

NAMELESS; WHAT A FOOL BELIEVES

There are thirty-two different species of rattlesnake that can be found in the United States. The smallest species, the aptly named pygmy rattlesnake, averages around twelve to fourteen inches, boasts vibrant dorsal splotches, and is very rarely fatal to humans. Chances are, though, when someone imagines a rattlesnake, it's the classic Western diamondback. Grayish brown scales the color of dirt, white lines outlining darker, hexagonal patches along its back, golden eyes in a permanent glare, venom easily capable of killing an adult human if left untreated. This breed tends to range from three feet to six feet in length and weighs about two to four pounds.

However, there's a breed of diamondback that can be found in the southeastern part of the country, and they're often a foot longer and several pounds heavier than their Western cousins. In fact, the largest rattlesnake ever recorded in the United States was an Eastern diamondback: over eight feet long and close to fifteen pounds of coiled, scaly muscle.

What begins to emerge, head first, from the bathroom ceiling vent isn't *that* large. But it *is* an Eastern diamondback, and not a small one. It's the sort of specimen a Snake and Spider House might display with special prominence, for children and adults alike to gasp at in fear.

Abe is gasping. His initial screams have turned into ghosts of themselves.

He's also weeping. A helpless, awed kind of weeping. Shaking his head. Moaning, "No, no, no, no."

The snake ignores Abe's refusals. It continues slowly and intractably outward. Not cautious, more like. . . skeptical. Maybe even annoyed.

Its tongue flicks out.

Scanning.

Probing.

Already, it's the size of Abe's hand and forearm, and there's no sense that the end of its body is anywhere near. Somewhere in the ceiling, its rattle whirs, ghosts of cicadas on a summer day.

In a few minutes, gravity will take over. Then, Abe understands, the snake will not be trapped in the room with him. He will be trapped in the room with it.

He picks up the plunger from where it fell during his spill to the floor and backs away as far as he can go. His left hand throbs harder and harder. His eyes never leave the snake, but he can feel the locked bathroom door in his peripheral vision, taunting him, pressing down on him like the compactor of a garbage truck.

His legs want to give out, but he wants as little of himself near the ground as possible.

When the snake finally drops down onto the wet tile floor, it makes a thunderous noise.

Like a heavy stone falling into a shallow puddle. Like a war drum played in the rain.

XXX

The snake swirls into an enormous coil where it landed, close to the toilet. No cute name for it, like Boris. It's too massive, too elemental for names. It stares back at Abe. Flickers its tongue at him.

"Oh God," Abe wheezes through a pinhole throat. He tries to appeal to the person in the ceiling once more. "Are you still up there? Please let me out? Please stop this? Please! Please, God, please!"

Oh, Bobbe says with a luxuriant sigh, *now you believe in God. Now you pray.*

He's barely even aware of the voice in his head. He's as close to actual disassociation as he's ever been.

Why is this happening?

What did he do to deserve this?

How can he hope to survive?

He doesn't know.

He doesn't know *anything.*

The crushed and curled body of Boris lays near his feet. So small now. Shrunken in death.

Will he look the same way? After his blood congeals in his veins? Will he land face first into that piss puddle and taste piss as he dies? Will he be eaten, or will he be left to rot, perhaps alongside the serpent that kills him? Do rattlesnakes eat their victims?

He doesn't know *fucking anything!*

Another voice pipes up in his head.

You don't have to be afraid of a stupid snake, man. You're a monster slayer! You defeated Boris the Spider with your bare hands! Even Frodo couldn't do that shit.

Usually Abe hates—or at least barely puts up with—Ty's Boy Scout enthusiasm. Now he's desperate for it. Even if he doesn't believe a word of it. There's no defeating what cannot be named.

The snake holds its rattle up and shakes it, agitated. The sound moves through Abe like an electric shock. The bathroom's too small; Abe can't back up any further and he's still too close for the snake's comfort.

"Go into the corner, you fuck," he growls. "You've got more room behind you."

The snake doesn't listen. Its head rises up a few inches and bobs back and forth. *Flicka-flick-flick*, its black tongue, a visual stutter.

It's going to strike.

He's seen random internet videos of how fast they launch themselves forward. Like horizontal lightning. He's also seen what rattlesnake venom does. It turns your blood into Thanksgiving cranberry sauce. The canned kind that slides onto the plate in a quivering lump.

It's going to hurt. A lot. He wants to cry. He wants to put the plunger down, sit, and sob about the unfairness of it all. All he'd wanted to do was take a leak and now—

Unfairness is the law of the world. Bobbe's voice again. *I tried to teach you that and you refused to listen. When I was a little gir—*

"Oh my God, SHUT UP!" Abe shouts—and without intending to, he stomps his foot in petulant rage.

The snake actually flinches a little. Shrinks back into itself. As surprised as Bobbe Medyl might be to hear Abe yell like this.

There you go, Monster Slayer, Ty says. *Scare that fucking snake!*

"SHUT UP, SHUT UP, SHUT *UP*," Abe shouts again. Aware that he might ultimately be making the snake more upset, but for this brief moment he doesn't care.

He starts stamping his feet and, without even thinking, he begins to huff out a death metal version of "What a Fool Believes."

"He came from some! Where! Ba-gg-ina! Long! A! Guh!" he shouts in a glottal growl that's half Michael McDonald, half Satan Himself.

The snake has no idea what to do with this.

Abe realizes that the toilet seat is up and an insane plan flashes in his mind: get the snake wrapped around the plunger and somehow get it into the bowl. Close the lid, sit on it if he has to, but get it in the bowl and out of his sight.

It's impossible. It's impractical. But it's also:

"WHAT A FOOL BELIEEEEVES!" he bellows. "HE SEES! THE WAH MAH HAH NAH POWER!"

He has to act fast, while the snake is confused. Jab it with the plunger like a snake handler.

Don't think, bro! Ty again. Just do it!

And he's about to. He really is.

Then he hears something at his feet. A *shhh* whisperrasping across the tile. He can't help but look down. Just for a microsecond.

Something has been slipped into the room from under the door.

A note.

Someone outside has passed him a note. What the absolute, everloving f—

He turns back just in time to see the rattlesnake launching itself towards him.

SNAKEBITE;
LONDON CALLING

It doesn't hurt like he thought it would. He supposes it's shock. His nerves need a moment to collect themselves before reporting on the agonizing end that's in store for his body. The clotting suffocation.

Then he realizes what actually happened.

The snake's aim was just a tiny bit off—or maybe Abe also happened to move the plunger as his body turned. Instead of Abe's flesh, the snake latched its fangs into the black plastic of the plunger.

Even a quarter of an inch in the other direction and its venom would be pulsing through Abe's chest right now.

Sheer, dumb luck.

That's all it was.

The plunger was in his dominant hand—the one not swelling up like a balloon animal right now—but when the snake's not-inconsiderable weight was added, the plunger fell out of his grip and clattered to the floor. Now the snake is writhing and twisting and Abe realizes its teeth are stuck in the thick plastic. It can't detach itself yet. He has to act fast.

Despite his nerves' shrieking protestations, Abe wraps both hands around the wooden dowel, avoiding the thrashing rattle like it's a scorpion's tail. With all his goddamn might, like Paul Simonon bringing his bass down onto the stage floor of the Palladium on the cover of *London Calling*, he starts slamming the snake against the wall. It doesn't do much damage; the softness of the plunger must be buffeting the blows. Abe can sense the snake's fangs beginning to wriggle free from the plastic, so he reverts back to plan A. He dashes towards the toilet.

Just as the snake's fangs finally escape the plunger, Abe manages to drape the snake over the rim of the bowl, with the snake's head dipping into the water. Before the fucker can squirm out, Abe slams the seats down onto the snake's upper back and then sits as hard as he can. The solid resistance of the reptile underneath is horrifying—a metal pipe wrapped in muscle. But after a few bounces up and down, really putting his weight into it, he feels something inside the snake break. Its rattle whips, spasms, twitches. . . and finally stills.

NOTES; THE BEST SONG YOU EVER HEARD; HANNUKAH PRESENT; THE PROCLAIMERS

Abe sits there for a long time.

Panting.

Sweating.

Tingling all over. Carbonated by adrenaline.

A long time.

Years, maybe.

What finally gets him to move is remembering the note on the floor. He stands up, amazed at how suddenly sore and tired his body is, and waddles his way to the door.

Before he picks the note up, he checks back with the snake. Definitely still dead. But unlike Boris, the snake seems to have grown in death. Abe can't believe how much of it trails out from the closed toilet lid. Like a giant necktie. Its defeat feels impossible. He should absolutely be dead now.

He gives a weak shout through the door, "Why are you doing this?" His voice sounds so small for such a mighty gladiator. "Hello? Will you just talk to me?" Then, absurdly, he tries: "I'm not mad. I promise."

Worth a shot. Might even be true. But like all his other attempts, it goes unanswered.

XXX

It turns out to not be a note. At least, not in the way Abe expected. The white piece of paper slid under the door had been folded in half to act as a simple envelope. When he picks it up, what looks like confetti rains down from inside.

No, not confetti. After he retrieves the bits that fell—grateful none of them fluttered over to the piss puddle—he sees they're five pieces of candy wrappers, each cut to show one letter, like a ransom note that had forgotten its glue.

Before he can indulge himself in thinking maybe this is all just some random garbage that happened to blow under the door, his brain puts together the word the letters are spelling. He even recognizes the source of each letter.

The Y is from a Hershey Bar.

The O is from an Almond Joy.

The U is from a bag of Sour Patch Kids.

The R is from a Snickers.

And the E is from a 3 Musketeers.

Abe suddenly feels very cold.

"I'm what?" he asks. "I'm *what?*" He pulls on the door. Pounds it with his good hand. Kicks it. He screams: "I'm WHAT?!"

But he knows the answer.

Doomed.

Fucked.

A goner.

Dead.

The suddenness with which he whips around almost makes him fall. He's *positive* the snake is moving.

It's not. It's still draped over the rim of the toilet bowl. Still totally immobile.

But there's that vent in the ceiling. Anything could come out of there next. And Abe is so tired. He's been lucky—

amazingly lucky—twice. No way he'll be lucky again a third time.

And his hand hurts so badly.

He's doomed. Fucked. A goner. Dead.

A memory tugs at the back of his brain. Some anecdote or lesson he'd heard about death. About already being dead.

He can't chase it down, though—instead, he gets distracted by another soft rasping noise across the floor.

A new note has been slid under the door.

"Fuck you!" Abe screams. "Why are you doing this to me?" No answer. "I'm not gonna play your fucking games, asshole! LET ME FUCKING OUTTA HERE!" His voice cracks. He sounds like he's going to cry. *Joke's on you*, he thinks, *I'm not going to cry*, and then feels the warmth of tears spilling down his cheeks again.

It only takes him a few moments to arrange the letters from this second note into a word. Longer than the first, but he's almost disappointed it's over so quickly. For those blissful seconds, his brain is occupied with something other than blank terror.

The G is from a bag of gummy bears;

The O from a Mr. Goodbar;

The N from a Crunch bar;

Another N from a bag of Corn Nuts;

And the A from a bag of Lays.

You're Gonna

"Die," he whispers. "The next one is going to say 'Die.'"

He has to wait a while to find out, sitting there, staring at the gap at the bottom of the door—but of course, he's already lost any real sense of time. It could be dawn, it could be the next evening, it could be fifteen minutes since he first discovered he was locked in. Darwin's Foëtus has a bit they love trotting out at gigs, called "Schrödinger's Pop Hit." Abe and Ty will talk about it in between every song, telling the crowd that it's their most popular song and that they'll get to it soon since they know it's what everyone is really there to hear. Then they'll finish their set and if anyone asked afterwards about why they didn't play that one song, they'll say, "But wasn't it the best song you ever heard?" Not quite nailing what Schrödinger was all about (and Ty could attest to this, given he actually majored in quantum physics), but it's all in good fun. After all, as long as the song remained unplayed it could exist as both the best song and not.

Now, I've been Schrödinger-ized, Abe thinks. *I'm living and dead. Just waiting for someone to open this box and find me in my true state.*

He tries to chuckle at the thought. Fails.

He also tries chasing down that earlier memory. Something about death being foregone, about brokenness being inevitable. It continues to elude him, but he thinks it has something to do with glass?

Doesn't matter. It won't help him. Nothing will.

Soon enough, one more white sheet of paper slips under the door, folded in half, pregnant with cutout letters.

Abe feels he doesn't even need to review the letters inside. There will be three squares and they'll spell out D-I-E.

Curiosity gets the better of him, though, and he peeks.

There are only two letters.

The B is from the sticky, cloying wrapper of a Honey Bun.

And the E is from a bag of Cheetos. The tiniest bit of residual orange dust still clings to the plastic.

"Huh?" he whispers. *You're gonna be. . . ?*

Gonna be what? Gonne *be* dead? Bad enough being tortured by a gleeful psychopath; does the grammar need to be tortured too? Or, worse: is his captor working towards quoting that damned Proclaimers song?

More time passes. Abe stands there, no longer able to think of anything other than what could be going on out there, what word could be next.

A strange, tangy, meaty smell seems to be emanating from under the door now. And did he just hear a faint, wet sloshing coming from the depths of the store? And giggling?

Eventually, another note appears.

This time Abe leaps for it, like it's a Hannukah present.

Before he opens it up, he notices a distressing detail. The white paper is smudged with dark red. Just a tiny bit, in the corner of one side of the ad hoc envelope.

Nope. I'm gonna be. . . ignoring that detail.

Four squares inside.

The letters are easily arranged, though not easily explained.

G, from a Good & Plenty box.

L, from a Jack Link's beef jerky.

A, from a bag of Smartfood Popcorn.

D, from a bag of Snyder's pretzels.

He hears a squeaking noise and assumes it comes from his own throat.

"Glad?" he whispers to himself. Baffled. "What am I going to be glad ab—?"

Then another noise—one that makes Abe bolt upright and spin around. A soft, brief, high pitched squeal coming from the airducts.

It could just be the air conditioning. Or it could be some gibbering horror, squeezing its way through the dark hole in the ceiling to join Abe in one more fight to the death.

You're gonna be glad you only met Boris and the snake so far.

Abe backs all the way up against the wall, heart hammering, mind spinning with all the nightmarish possibilities.

Somehow, what happens next is worse than anything he could imagine.

The lights cut out.

Abe is plunged into complete darkness.

THE HAIRLIP MAN

Now the room is full of noises: a wail, a sob, a moan, a cry. All Abe.

Not the dark, please, don't leave me in the dark where I can't even see what's about to come out of the ceiling next, no, no, no—

He shuts up once he realizes someone is also standing in the room with him.

There, in the corner. On the opposite side of this tiny, dark room.

Abe can't see anything, but he can definitely feel the unmistakable presence of another human body.

He can also hear breathing—not his, someone else's. He holds his own panicky, keening breaths just to be sure, and—yes. Someone else is breathing in here. No doubt about it. *Oh God.*

A fear he hasn't felt so keenly since childhood stabs into him.

The Hairlip Man.

The Hairlip Man is in here with him.

The Hairlip Man is going to watch as whatever drops next out of the vent finally fills Abe with enough poison to coagulate his blood and kill him. The Hairlip Man will smile his secret, charming smile while Abe dies in the dark.

For all her complaining and kvetching and reveling in the misery that was her life, Bobbe Meydl never went into too much detail about the incidents that had traumatized her as a child. She liked to keep it vague and mysterious: "If you knew the things that had happened to me when I was a little girl in Poland. . ."

But there was one detail she'd shared with Abe.

He'd been seven years old. For reasons he can't remember, Bobbe was staying with them for a few days, sleeping in his room while he slept in a pillow fort out in the living room. He'd been so excited about this new arrangement—he loved forts, and he loved the living room because that's where the television was.

The only problem was, he was coming off of a series of weeks where he'd been having terrible nightmares. Midnight shriekfests that sent him running to his mom's room for comfort.

It had been long enough since he'd had one of these night terrors that he'd kind of forgotten about them, in the way only children can do. Something about sleeping in a new location must have brought them surging back.

Instead of running to his mom's, though, he ran to his own room. Weeping, terrified, desperate for the familiar. Bobbe Meydl was sitting up on his bed, blinking sleep from her eyes.

"You have nothing to be afraid of," she'd said, after he'd breathlessly reported what had happened. Lest he think she was trying to comfort him, she followed up with: "You don't know what being afraid really is."

Abe had been defiant, though. "I do! I know all about monsters!" Suddenly it was imperative to him that he convince her. He began rattling off all the scary movies he'd seen (or, more accurately, heard about at school). Freddy and Jason and Chucky and, and, and.

She listened, face pulled in its usual perma-scowl, eyes glittering with smugness. When he finished, she smoothed his hair. He'll never forget the tingle that sped through his body when she did so—that desperate appreciation of her physical attention.

"This is how I know you're a child, boychik," she said. "Your monsters are ridiculous. They are circus clowns. When evil comes, Abraham, it does not wear a mask. It looks as plain as day. I was a little girl when I learned that. The Hairlip Man. . ."

She trailed off. He demanded she tell him what the phrase meant.

She stared at him, then said, "I don't know if he was a Russian or a German. I only know he was so handsome. Except for that one tiny detail, which made his face memorable. I memorized his face as I watched him do what he did to my mother. As he loomed over me. As he chased me into the woods."

The Hairlip Man.

Abe felt his eyes going wide. Felt a different kind of chill spreading through his body. He didn't even know what a hairlip was—let alone that it was really spelled *harelip*—but it conjured surreal, horrible beauty.

Perhaps she would've told him more, if his mom hadn't come in then, yelling at his grandmother to stop, to not tell little Abe "that story."

Bobbe Meydl had received her daughter's outrage with a grin—a devilishly delighted one, Abe thought later. She liked scaring her grandson. "I had to live through it—he can't bear to hear it from the safety of his pillows?"

He never thought to ask for more details later on. She'd told him enough. The Hairlip Man was firmly planted in his brain from then on. For the next several years—up until high school, really—whenever Abe had another shriekfest in the dark, it was because the Hairlip Man had come for him at last, the fine hairs that made up his lips rippling like underwater kelp.

Now he knows: the Hairlip Man has found him again.

glad glad i'm going to be glad i should be glad because i'm not going to die alone he's going to be here with me in the dark and

"Shut up."

Abe hears the voice next to his ear, as real as the pain in his hand, the aches in his muscles.

"Shut *up.*"

The voice is sharp, like a slap to the face. He physically twitches when he hears it. Then it became deliberate, without sympathy, like hands squeezing a throat shut.

"Don't let him win. *Think.*"

He heeds this strange, new voice and shuts up. Takes a steadying breath—which is still very much unsteady. Tries to think.

What are his options? If he lets himself stand here, panic churning in his chest like a hot tub gone haywire, imagining what might be pouring out of the ceiling vent, he's gonna literally lose his mind. He might wind up bashing his brains out on the wall or floor like one of those desperate orcas he heard about, purposefully ramming their snouts into their tank to escape their amusement park prisons.

But what to do about the person in here with him, watching him? Can he really hope to fight a human blind when fighting just a spider in full light took so much out of him? He's an out-of-shape bassist—what will he do when this stranger is suddenly next to him, grabbing him, *touching* him—

"No one's in here and you know it," that other, sharper voice insists, and then he realizes—it's *himself* who's speaking. Bobbe's no-love attitude, but out of his throat. "You've been staring at every inch of this bathroom for at least a couple hours now—how would anyone have gotten in without you noticing?"

That's true. He doesn't *believe* it, but he can't argue with it.

Regardless, there's still the matter of other critters dropping from the vent to join him. That's a *very* plausible threat.

First thing to do, then: make his eyes adjust as much as possible. He squeezes them shut, counts to five, and when he opens them again, he's able to see a little bit more than before.

Better. As far as he can tell nothing is skittering towards him yet. The light coming from under the door helps a little bit too, and—

Looking down at that crack of light, he notices something white and rectangular on the floor.

Another note.

At first, the usual dread surges through him at the thought of what new word in this torturous puzzle waits for him to decipher. Then, a more confounding thought:

Why would the person tormenting him slip him a note and *then* cut the power so he can't read it? Abe was obviously being held by a psychopath, but that? That just doesn't make *sense*.

He thinks back to what happened the moments before the lights cut out.

"Wait. . ."

He slaps his hands against the wall behind him until he feels the telltale ridges and shapes of a light switch.

He flicks the switch in the opposite direction.

The fluorescents blink back on. A sickly yellow, blue stuttering that makes his eyes water a little.

"Son of a bitch," he says in a shocked gasp. "Goddammit."

The laughter comes first. Great gales of it. Laughter until his abs hurt.

Then come the sobs. They burble out of him in hitching, gulping waves. He tries to quiet them down as quickly as they arise, but somehow that makes them even stronger. He's at their mercy until they finally ebb a few minutes later.

"Son of a bitch," he says again, wiping the tears and snot with his forearm.

Ever mindful of the vent in the ceiling, he walks over to the sink and splashes some water on his face.

He makes brief eye contact with his tear-puffed face in the mirror and then immediately looks away. He's feeling relief. He's feeling embarrassment. He's feeling anger—fury, even—at how vulnerable he is in this fucking room. But underneath all these things, he's feeling something which scares him and disturbs him and keeps him from being able to look at himself.

Gratitude.

A warped kind of gratitude.

Being trapped in the dark caused a level of fear he'd never felt spike through his body. When the lights came back on, when he realized it had just been a mistake and that his captor was trying to kill him and/or drive him insane, *but at least wasn't leaving him alone in the dark,* Abe felt grateful for that bit of kindness.

"Jesus fucking Chruuuuh," he mutters. He wants to puke.

There's a toilet right there, bro, he imagines Ty saying, and if there wasn't the dead body of a large rattlesnake draped inside, he might take the opportunity.

Aren't rattlesnakes still dangerous after they're dead?

Abe vaguely recalls more random shit from the internet. Texas farmers sent to the hospital because of bite reflexes from dead snakes or something. Doesn't matter. The toilet is off limits for the sheer gag factor alone. If he has to puke *over* that horrible snake body he might never stop.

No puking. Just thinking. Puke later. Survive to puke another day.

That new note on the floor beckons him.

He goes over to pick it up, but stops when he reaches the light switch by the door. He gives the room one last suspicious look.

"I really thought someone was in here with me," he mumbles.

Bobbe answers—in her own voice this time.

Fear will do that. Fear makes you stupid.

But it wasn't just fear or him being stupid. It was the *breathing*. He would have sworn he'd heard breathing.

Partially as an experiment and partially to just confirm what had happened, Abe reaches over and turns out the lights again.

Perfect darkness.

Perfect silence.

No breathing noises this time.

Had Abe imagined the breathing before? In the same way his eyes had imagined the shape of a (*Hairlip*) man in the corner?

Or maybe . . . had his captor been on the other side of this door, listening? Breathing heavily?

Whoever is trapping me in here is very interested in what I do.

How can I use that against him?

Abe turns the lights back on.

Then he bends down to pick up the note, curious to see what he's supposed to be so glad about.

HEARTS HEARTS HEARTS
HEARTS HEARTS

No ransom note letters this time.

No familiar snack food labels turned into diverting jumbles.

Just four simple words, followed by an array of crudely simple hearts, handwritten in what Abe really, *really* hopes is reddish brown ink.

you
stayed
in
there!
♥ ♥ ♥ ♥ ♥

You're Gonna Be Glad You Stayed In There

Abe runs the sentence over in his head again and again. He thinks he understands what it's implying, but he just can't let himself believe it. There has to be some other, deeper meaning.

You're Gonna Be Glad You Stayed In There...

That implies he's going to be let out. It might even imply. . .

"No," he whispers. "Don't fucking mean that."

Thinking of how he'd simply had to turn the lights back on to escape the darkness, he puts a trembling hand on the doorknob.

You're Gonna Be Glad You Stayed In There. . .

"Please, fucking, *no.*"

He turns the knob and gives the door the faintest of pushes.

You're Gonna Be Glad You Stayed In There. . .

The door gives way. Just a crack for now, but he can tell there's no resistance.

God help me.

The deadbolt outside has been disengaged.

The door is unlocked.

How long had it been unlocked?

How long has he been able to escape?

Before he pushes the door open all the way, though, another question comes to him. The million dollar one.

(*you're gonna be glad you stayed*)

Should he?

He steps outside.

XXX

As with the giant spider, Abe's first thought is this must be a prank.

The entire convenience store—so shiny, so immaculate when he'd first come in—is slathered in red. Not an inch untouched.

Someone must have screwed in a couple of those novelty boudoir bulbs or something. Or maybe heat lamps? Is that why I'm sweating so hard?

Two things prevent his brain from buying into such nonsense.

All the clumps of darker, blacker, wetter red.

And the stench, which hits him like a physical wall. That thick, meaty smell, dialed up to a million.

The convenience store has been bathed, drenched, literally painted in blood.

Organs are dumped haphazardly across the floor and on shelves.

Other, larger masses reveal themselves to be human bodies—at least three of them, nude and slumped in undignified positions.

Abe's throat closes as his gorge rises. He wants to cry, vomit, eject any and everything from his body onto the floor, and hey, why not: insides are apparently meant for the outside in this hellish abattoir.

His brain keeps processing details of the scene. Like what looks like a set of lungs draped over the coffee machines. Or a semi-deflated eyeball resting below the nozzle of one of the Icee dispensers. Or the arcing streaks that tell him the blood must have been literally mopped onto the floor and slathered across the walls and beverage cases. He even remembers those faint sloshing sounds from earlier. Which means, somewhere, there's probably a mop bucket full of—

Stop looking. Just move. Get out of here.

Yes. Good idea. As far as he can tell, no one else is currently here with him. His path to the front door looks unimpeded. In fact, he can see his car from here. Just on the other side of the glass front of the building.

He moves as quickly, quietly, carefully as he can. His shoes stick and squelch, leaving thick prints in the red underneath.

His eyes fall on the nearest body, posed face down and ass up against one of the beverage refrigerators. Several long objects protrude like tail feathers from its rear. The ice scrapers, plunged in deep.

Are these bodies real? Do they belong to the owners of the other cars outside? Or employees of the store? No way to know.

He stares a moment too long, waiting to see if there's any movement. Any survivors—or, worse, anyone *pretending* to be dead, like in that one *Saw* movie. . .

Another detail. One he really wishes he wasn't beginning to see. The body he's looking at isn't red because it was painted with blood like the floors. That's the corrugation of muscle.

Much of this person's skin has been removed.

Abe almost retches again.

Okay, really *time to go.*

He's about to break into a run when, on the other side of the store, the door to the backroom opens and someone comes through, dragging a heavy bulk that can only be another corpse.

Abe freezes.

The corpse-dragger drops the newest body to the blood-slick floor, gives their own lower back a stretch, and turns around.

Hard to say for sure, but based on size and shape, Abe assumes the figure is male. Dressed in all black. Form fitting black pants. A long sleeve black shirt.

His head is covered in holes.

Fathomless, black holes, honeycombed in row upon row across what should be the stranger's face.

Abe's stomach plummets.

"Oh!" the hole-faced stranger exclaims, voice bright and cheery. "I was wondering when you'd come out! Didja see all this?"

He gestures to the room. When he moves, the holes on his face waggle slightly, and Abe quickly understands they're not holes. They're huge, dilated pupils.

Googly eyes. Affixed to some sort of mask.

That mask has a strange glow around the edges, but Abe doesn't get a chance to observe further. Laughing like a loon, the eyeball-man suddenly breaks into a full sprint, bolting right for Abe.

Abe feels his mind yank apart in two directions—run for the door! run for safety!—and his body takes over. He turns for the closest option, the most familiar.

He barely makes it back to the bathroom in time. He slams the door shut behind him and engages the handle lock, just as his whooping, guffawing pursuer collides with the metal on the other side. The door rattles in its frame, but the handle lock holds.

More thuds. More maniacal laughter.

"I saw you! I SAWWWWW YOU! Hooo! Hooo!"

A small shape skitters in from under the door.

Abe flinches and kicks it into a corner.

Another googly eye. Staring up at the ceiling.

The laughter continues.

Abe can only back further into the bathroom, joining the dead spider, the dead snake, and sob in response.

RESCUE AT LAST;
ANOTHER ESCAPE ROUTE

The cops finally—finally—show up sometime later.

The unmistakable whoop of sirens announces their arrival—sounding almost like mask-muffled laughter at first.

Then Abe sees red and blue lights under the crack in the door.

He hears indistinguishable shouts. The comforting melody of authority. The percussive rattle of gunfire. The silence that follows.

"I'm coming out!" Abe shouts. "Don't shoot!"

He opens the bathroom door and sees the eyeball-man sprawled on the bloody ground. Body riddled with bullet holes, like a mocking replica of his mask.

Officers stand over the psychopath, guns still smoking. Other officers flood into the store.

One notices Abe. "Put your hands up!" the officer shouts, but Abe is already complying, grateful tears running down his face.

The cops see that Abe's no threat and usher him out of the store into the blissfully muggy night. They wrap arms around his shoulders and the feeling of comfort is exquisite.

Not as exquisite as the sight that greets him outside, though.

He has to blink several times before he can really process it. The strobing lights from all the vehicles makes it hard to see. But once his eyes adjust, there can be no doubt.

Jenna is here. Waiting for him. Her own face, tear-streaked, as well.

"I was so worried," she says, and runs to him, wrapping her arms around him in a desperate hug.

"What—?" All Abe can do is stammer. "How—?"

She gives a wet laugh, wiping at her eyes before placing her hands on his cheeks as if she can't believe he's really real. "They traced your phone. Because you were using your map, they were able to reverse the satellite feed and find out where you were."

"That's" (*impossible*) "amazing," he says.

"You're amazing," she says, and kisses him. Her lips are firm but soft and sweetly flavored with tobacco. Heavenly. He breathes her in. If he could just smell her upper lip for-ever, every moment up to this point would have been worth it.

"But wait," he asks, pulling away, hating himself for breaking the moment. "How did they even know to start looking for me? And why are you here with them?"

Jenna's eyes search his. Her heart-stopping eyes, framed so perfectly by lashes as alluring as sea anemones.

"Oh, baby," she sighs, and pulls him close to whisper in his ear. "Because you're daydreaming."

"What?" He blinks.

He's back in the bathroom.

Sitting on the floor opposite the door.

The body of the spider, the snake, the puddle of piss, the glaring fluorescent light.

"You're daydreaming," she says again. Only, the voice isn't coming from his head. . . is it? His ears are ringing—a constant, high shriek from the stress of everything—so he can't tell for sure. But, just like when he was trapped in darkness, he's almost positive he's hearing a voice from outside his skull.

It's not coming from his own throat this time, though. This time, it sounds like it's coming from. . .

The mirror?

"You're daydreaming, stupid."

He can't see the mirror from where he's sitting, but the direction of the voice is unmistakable. So's the tenor of the speaker. It's not Jenna; it's his grandmother.

He sighs.

"Eat shit, Bobbe," he mutters back. Actually out loud. Who cares? Let him sound crazy. This might be the last conversation he ever has.

"*You're* the one eating shit," she says. "You're pathetic. Running away. You could've made it to that front door. You *chose* to be trapped."

"No, I didn't."

"Yes, you did."

"He could've followed me outside! He could've gotten me before I even got to the front door!"

"You're telling yourself that."

"Can you maybe try having empathy for once in your miserable life? Why are you always such a judgmental. . ." He holds back. Calling his grandmother a bitch seems like a heresy that can't be undone, even if it's all just in his head.

"See?" He can hear her smug grin. "Weak."

"I can't just run at him. I need a weapon or something."

"Your mind is your best weapon."

"Great. Lemme just scoop that out and throw it at him like a fucking water balloon."

"Excuses, excuses, always with the excuses. 'I can't do this; I can't do that.' You've been trapped by that *shtusim* well before you found this bathroom."

Abe squeezes his eyes shut. Arguing with a mirror. Bobbe's right about one thing: he's pathetic.

Then, suddenly, an idea. That dim anecdote about broken glass. He still can't remember the specifics of it, but. . .

His eyes pop open and he leaps to his feet, pulling off his overshirt and wrapping it around his not-broken fist.

His grandmother is still in the mirror, castigating him, mocking him, decrying him—him and his entire worthless generation. Great. Let her. Just makes it all the easier to—

Crack!

A single punch to the glass leaves a spiderweb in the center. It actually feels exquisite to hit something.

Crack, crack, crack!

A few more blows and several shards loosen and fall to the ground.

He picks up the largest with his wrapped hand.

"I've got a weapon now," he says.

Shut his grandma up too.

Or is she simply daring him to put his money where his mouth, his wrapped fist, might be?

He looks at the door.

"Fuck all y'all," he whispers to no one.

Do it. Do it now. He won't be expecting it, and you've got a weapon.

"Yeah. I do."

But the memory of that awful, hooting laughter, the grisly decorations. . . Now that a psychical confrontation is guaranteed, Abe is frozen in his tracks. He finds himself staring at that solitary googly eye on the floor.

When evil comes, Abraham, it won't be wearing a mask...

Well, this time it definitely fucking *is*. And look how many other people are dead already. Eyeball Guy's clearly got psycho-strength. What if he also has a gun? That'd drop Abe well before he can get into shard-wielding range. It's good he's found something in this bathroom he can use to defend himself, but it's not like he's suddenly invincible.

Strategy. Think. Is there a way to avoid running into the guy. A way to avoid—(*those awful eyes*)—being seen?

He tears his gaze away from the plastic eye on the floor, looks around his all-too-familiar prison. His sights land on the ceiling vent.

He'd heard someone crawling around up there, before Boris and the snake were dropped down. Which means someone was able to get up there. Which means...

He looks at the rest of the ceiling panels. Reachable, if he stands on something.

Something like the toilet.

Maybe there's another escape route that's been available to him this whole time.

SPECIMEN; INVINCIBILITY STAR; MURDERER

"Dude." Ty's voice, coming from one of the mirror shards on the floor. "How is this a better plan than just running out and fighting the guy?"

Abe ignores him, focusing instead on balancing on the toilet.

"Careful of that snake! Remember—"

"I know," Abe grunts in reply. "Posthumous bite reflex."

"Good name for a song, right? I read online that those fuckers can still bite hours after death, and they're still chock full of poison."

"It's venom," Abe mutters back. "And you only know that because *I* know that, because you're just a fucking voice in my head."

"Ouch, dude."

Both toilet lids are closed on top of the snake's body, but it barely compacts under Abe's weight. He rocks unsteadily on tiptoes, having wild thoughts of princesses and peas.

He could just pull the snake out and throw it in a corner, but he doesn't want to look at the fanged mouth of that thing ever again. It's okay. He can balance.

He takes a breath before pushing up one of the popcorn panels above him. His entire body feels clenched in a pre-emptive wince, too aware there could be any number of other spiders and snakes waiting up here—legless horrors and horrors with too many legs. That said, nothing else has made an appearance through the vent since the rattlesnake, so he's reasonably confident nothing is waiting for him.

He's half correct. In the darkness above, nothing crawls out to surprise him, but he *can* make out two brown boxes around the panels nearest the vent. On the nearest box, he makes out some words stamped on the side—*"Trumbull Farms"* and *"specimen transport"*—and shivers a little in recognition. Boris' and the snake's. Presumably, at the very least, empty now.

Abe tries to scan the rest of the shadowy landscape. If this is going to be a viable option, he'll need to find a way out of the convenience store that's ideally not the same way his tormentor used.

However, that means he needs to lift himself higher to see further into the ceiling space. Which also means inserting more of his face into the dark realm of the New Trumbull Farms.

A quick prayer to any deity within prayershot.

He plants his elbows into the joints of the ceiling panel and lifts.

The effort of holding himself up like this is agonizing. The uneven toilet lids rock under his tiptoes. He won't be able to balance like this for long. He clumsily rotates himself around to get a better sense of the landscape.

Another box is staring him right in the face. It had been behind his head this whole time.

Several spiders and a thick, centipede-looking monstrosity crawl along its side. Not empty at all. And barely two inches from his nose.

"Fuck!" He hisses. Flails. Tries to shove the box away. His legs kick impotently, toes searching for purchase. In the shuffling, he accidentally puts too much weight on the nearest ceiling panel and it gives way. Down it—and he—goes.

He plummets to the hard tile floor, narrowly missing cracking his back on the toilet.

The pain is symphonic, but tempered by the realization that he'd succeeded in tilting that surprise box towards the now-busted ceiling panel and it's currently raining insects onto him. Spiders. Centipedes. God knows what else. He can hear their horrid bodies plinking against the floor, into the piss puddle. He can feel hundreds of legs scrambling against his skin, settling into his hair.

It's too much.

He bolts to his feet, swatting and stomping, not giving any creature a chance to bite him first. A merciless killing machine.

He hears himself scream-singing again, beyond hysterical this time—is he reciting Doobie Brothers lyrics? Billy Joel? Cannibal Corpse? He doesn't even know. It's just words and howling.

He used to hate killing bugs. Not just because they grossed him out, but because he always felt guilty killing anything that had an instinct to save its own life. Even cockroaches. He always assumed this was a side effect of Jewish guilt. An entire religion founded on constantly escaping near-extinction—how could you approach killing another living thing cavalierly?

Now, those thoughts are galaxies away from his mind. All he can think is kill, kill, kill. Leave nothing uneradicated.

Sometime later, the scream-singing comes to an end. He stands victorious, gasping for breath, surrounded by the bodies of his demolished foes. Nothing stirs in the room besides him. And, granted, he might not feel it even if he were, but he doesn't think he's bitten anywhere.

A miracle. And something even better: right now, he feels fucking invincible.

He feels like Mario after touching a star. He feels like he just got off the stage after a particularly cathartic and well-received scream-fest, not a single wrong note played.

Now! Go, now!!

His panting breaths come out like growls.

Not wasting a second, even to think about what he's doing, he tightens his grip on the mirror shard and yanks opens the bathroom door.

The guy in the eyeballs-mask isn't in sight. Abe strides purposefully and speedily towards the front door. Shoves it open. He feels like he can see in all directions right now, and like even the goddamn ocean would part for him.

The night air is the most beautiful feeling he's ever felt. He could almost cry. But not yet—crying will be reserved for later. He can feel his invincibility starting to waver, his legs starting to shake.

He heads straight for his car, then almost jumps when he notices: the van's gone. Its empty spot in the parking lot is as surreal and uncanny as an expert magic trick.

Did the guy up and leave? One last mindfuck?

No matter. Abe pats his pockets and for a moment thinks he doesn't have his keys, but then they're in his hand and he's fumbling with the unlock button on the key fob. Everything is working out exactly as it needs to. Almost done with this nightmare.

He's just about to open the driver's side door when a hand touches his shoulder.

"Help—" a soft voice whispers.

Abe's manic invincibility surges back. Still not even sure any of this is really happening, he spins around with (*snake-*

like) speed and starts mercilessly pumping his shard of glass into the unwelcome stranger's guts.

ASSAILANT; AN UNLUCKY KID; NO SURVIVORS; SELF-DEFENSE

"stop. . . stop please. . ."

It's the weakness of the voice, not the resistance of flesh against fist, nor the hot blood gushing over his hand, that clues Abe in that this is real, not another daydream.

He would never daydream someone making such desperate pleas.

He stops stabbing. Takes a step backwards, along the side of his car, to get a better look at his assailant.

Assailant. That's rich. You're the one who just ventilated his torso.

He's looking at a young man. A kid, really—probably only a year or two out of high school.

Thin. All elbows and Adam's apple. A faint spray of acne. A mop of unruly hair. Huge, innocent eyes. Even huger now, in their shock.

The kid is hunched over, holding his stomach where Abe just introduced a new series of speed holes, but Abe is able to see the kid is wearing baggy jeans and a loose, red and white polo shirt that bears the gas station's logo on the upper-left of the chest.

A loose black backpack was slung over the kid's right shoulder; now it droops off of his elbow.

"Sorry," the kid wheezes. His voice is high and reedy. Barely pubescent. "I'm—"

He collapses against the car.

Almost instinctively, Abe steps forward to catch the kid before he hits the ground. He's babbling apologies, too.

"No," the kid manages in a high, quavery voice. "My fault. I shouldn't have snuck up on you, I was just. . . stuck in the storeroom so long, I was so glad to see some—ohhh, God."

He loses his ability to speak in a wave of wooziness. His eyes roll up, revealing the whites. Abe thinks he might even pass out, but the kid manages to stay conscious with obvious effort.

"Fuck," Abe says. "You're hurt bad. Um. Fuck!"

The clerk's midsection is slick with blood. He's so heavy. Almost dead weight already.

"Did you see him?" The clerk asks. "The. . . eyeballs?"

"Yeah."

"Any. . . other survivors?"

"No."

The clerk gives a wheezy laugh. "I woulda done the same thing." He hisses in pain clutches at his stomach wounds. "So stupid. . . Didn't want to make too much noise, so I didn't yell first. I'm really sorry."

"Stop apologizing! I'm the one who's—I've gotta help you. We gotta get you to a hospital."

"Feeling. . . dizzy. . ."

He's probably losing too much blood. He might not even make it to a hospital. Shit. Fucking shit.

Leave him, his grandmother hisses in his head. *You're so close.*

"We've gotta stop the bleeding." Abe's eyes fall back on the convenience store. "There are bandages and stuff in there." Abe doesn't move, though. Not yet. Because. . . well, what if this is a trap?

The clerk looks at him, bent over his wounds. His eyes are so big and brimming with tears. It's as if he reads Abe's mind.

"You don't know me, man. Just go. Get help. Save yourself. *Please*." He looks at least three shades whiter already. Like he's literally draining in front of Abe. Ashen circles above his cheekbones. His acne-haunted face slick with sweat.

Abe looks at his car. Looks at the man—the kid!—he might have just murdered. Looks at where the CR8H8 van *used* to be.

Don't you DARE, Abraham.

The clerk echoes his grandmother's sentiments.

"Don't." Voice cracking like a goddamn thirteen-year-old. He clutches Abe's arm with one bloody hand. "Please. Get out of here while you can."

The kid's hand feels so small against Abe's arm. So light. So desperate for Abe to be selfish. To be like his goddamn, awful grandmother. But what's the point of surviving if he sacrifices his damned humanity to do it?

"Hey," Abe says, breaking free of the kid's grip without difficulty and holding up his glass shard. "I can defend myself." He gives the kid a pained grin. "Or didn't you notice?"

HUMANITY; BULKWARK;
UNEXPECTED CONTACT

Stupid, he thinks. *Stupid. Stupid. Stupid. Stupid.*

It should only take, like, ninety seconds tops to sneak in, grab bandages, and sneak back out. But time has begun to pull itself out like taffy.

Every squeak of his shoes against the blood-slick floor becomes a nine-part symphony.

Every heartbeat becomes an extended drum solo.

Every breath, an open invitation for the door to the employee area to swing back open again and reveal the masked psychopath.

Where are the bandages? Why are there so many food products? Who needs this many goddamn snacks?

He can feel dozens upon dozens of eyes on him. In fact, peripherally, he notices one or two more of those damned googly eyes on the floor, where they must've fallen off of their mask or something.

His own eyes are busy darting to the backroom door, to the bodies on display. He's waiting for something to move, to give him another cheap horror movie jump scare and come bolting straight for him.

The killer must be preoccupied skinning another victim or violating a corpse with automotive accessories, though. Or maybe he really did take his murder van and flee the scene.

All is silent and still.

Unbearably silent and still.

And the open door to the bathroom gapes like an audience member shocked and delighted to see Abe has returned.

At last Abe finds what he's looking for—why would health supplies be kept in the same aisle as antifreeze?!—and he fills his arms up and hurries back out into the night air, back tingling with the cold fire insistence that someone or something is behind him.

When he finds himself outside again, there comes that surprising feeling of invincibility once more. A giddiness. He's *alive*, goddammit.

Alive and with his humanity intact.

XXX

The van is gone, he keeps repeating in his head—a bulwark against panic.

The van is gone. The van is gone. The van is gone. The van is gone.

After ninety seconds in the convenience store, he gives himself two minutes to get the clerk bandaged up so he'll survive the trip to a hospital. This is an unconscionably risky thing to be doing—the sort of thing he's screamed at a thousand horror movie protagonists for doing on a thousand screens—but he can't stop himself. The clerk is acting like he's gonna bleed out otherwise.

"Keep a lookout for me," Abe tells him, while ripping open the bandages.

The young clerk gives a weak, but genuine laugh. "Just don't... tell me to 'keep my eyes peeled.'"

"Ugh. That fucking mask, right?"

The kid grimaces—maybe with pain or maybe with loathing. "I don't know if I'll ever unsee it."

Abe moves as quickly as he can. He's done all he can to mitigate the risk of staying here for these additional few moments. He's sitting in the driver's seat; the clerk is in the passenger seat. The keys are in the ignition. The engine is on and the convenience store is in full view. They're ready to peel out at the first twitch of danger—or the first sound of that horrible van returning.

Getting the kid into the car had been no easy task. He's not a large young man, but he was so weak it took both of their best efforts to get him seated. In fact, Abe's a little dismayed at how sapped his own energies have become. His adrenaline is ebbing.

Now, the clerk is leaning back to give Abe easier access to the gashes across his midsection. While the kid talks, Abe cleans and bandages up his wounds.

It had been a slow night, the clerk explains. "I was working in the backroom on stock stuff, which I hate, so I had my earphones in. Took me a while before I realized someone was shouting in the store. I came out to see what was going on—some... *guy* had come in. Wearing that mask. All those eyeballs. And he was yelling. There were two other customers and two employees, and he was yelling at all of them, almost like, like a preacher. He was saying he'd come to show them his 'creation.' He wanted to 'create' for them, whatever that means."

Abe swallows. He hears his throat click. "Hate," he says. "He wants to create hate."

The clerk looks at him with his wide, wet eyes that seem to say, that makes perfect sense.

"What happened next?" Abe asks.

"Well, that's when I noticed he had this knife. The biggest knife in the world. And he was blocking the front door, so no one could get past him. He slashed one of the customers. Then he threw the knife at another customer." He gestures to the spot between his eyebrows. "It just. . . sunk in. Never seen anything like it outside of a movie before. Trevor, one of the other clerks, tried to wrestle him down to the ground. He was too fast. Too strong. He started choking Trevor. And that *wasn't* like anything I'd seen in a movie before. Choking in a movie is slow and quiet. This was, like. . ." His voice fills with tears. "I thought his fingers were going to sink right through Trevor's neck. I. . . I wanted to do something, but I was so scared. I was frozen."

The kid looks off to the side, ashamed.

Abe wants to tell him he knows how he feels; instead, he lets the clerk continue, rapt.

"Then all those eyes pointed right at me. He let go of Trevor and he just *rushed* at me. Full speed. Laughing, this high, awful laugh. Then he shoved me. Never been shoved so hard. I don't know if it was against a wall or the floor, but I slammed my head. Blacked out. When I woke up, I was in the backroom and everything was super quiet. There was a Post-it Note on me. Right here on my chest. It said, '*Enjoy!*' With a buncha hearts. I came out and saw. . . everything he'd done." He fights back a wave of nausea.

Abe has finished applying bandages. The wounds actually didn't look so bad once all the blood was wiped away. The kid pulls his shirt down, wincing, and smooths it out. "Thank you. Think you just saved my life."

"Yeah, well. We're not outta the woods yet."

They both look at the store. The blood inside glistens like shellac.

"Why is it so quiet now?" the clerk asks. "Where do you think he went?"

Abe shrugs. "Maybe he... did what he wanted to do? Created what he wanted to create?" Abe realizes they're whispering. As if they're trying not to summon the monster back.

"You think he left us alive on purpose?"

Abe considers that. "What's the point of creation with no one there to witness it?"

The sight is almost hypnotic in its grisliness. Still lit up like an oasis in the dark.

Then his eyes focus on the bug guts, still smeared across the windshield. Splat. He snaps out of his reverie. They can't have been sitting here for longer than three or four minutes, but that's too long by half.

"Doesn't matter," he says. "We're outta here. And we're—What?"

"Your phone," the clerk says, pointing.

Abe had been so busy tending to the kid's wounds, his story, that he'd forgotten about his phone. His goddamn, piece of shit phone, plugged into the dash in its stupid little cradle.

It's ringing.

Someone is calling him *right now*.

The name on the caller ID makes Abe actually gasp.

"Who is it?" the clerk asks. He still seems weak, but his energy is returning. He's not as pale.

"One sec. Just... keep your eyes peeled."

Abe fumbles with the phone. He should be speeding away, calling the cops, but... this will only take a second. No internal voice tells him he's being stupid this time. Every character in his brain understands he needs to answer this call.

To confirm this is happening. To hear her voice.

"Jenna?" he asks, barely able to speak her name.

"Abe!" Jenna shouts on the other end. "Holy fuck, are you okay? We've been losing our minds over here!"

When he hears his name out of her mouth, he immediately breaks down in sobs.

But even through those sobs, he can hear her—really, truly, *actually her.*

She's rambling about how his brother has been wondering where he is, and so he called Ty and then Ty called her—everyone is worried. Abe has been MIA for hours and hours. Ty and Abe's brother decided maybe Abe got cold feet and was ghosting them, but Jenna—"you know how I'm a chronic insomniac"—volunteered to keep calling and see if she could get an answer.

"I dunno," she continues, "I just had a bad feeling. Like, something in the air. Like, you needed help."

She cares about him. She's attuned to him. How insane, after all he's gone through, that this is what his mind latches onto.

Still. No time.

"I—I—I can't talk right now, Jenna," he finally manages. "I'm at a gas station. I don't know where. By, um—" A name he'll never forget comes to him. "—Trumbull Farms' Snake and Spider House. If you look that place up, you'll know where I am, just a couple miles away."

"Trumbull Farms?"

"Yeah. Someone tried to kill me. For hours and hours."

"What?! Are you—?!"

"I'm still in danger, so I gotta go. I gotta call the cops. Maybe you call them too? I gotta get distance. But. . . But it's gonna be okay, Jenna. I think I can believe that now. It's really good to hear your voice."

"Wait, but—"

Somehow, the hardest thing he's done yet tonight is hang up on her. But he does it.

Before he puts the car in reverse, he wipes at his eyes. Takes a deep breath.

"Wow. You really love her."

The clerk's voice comes from a million miles away. Abe actually almost forgot he wasn't alone in the car.

"Love? I. . . I don't know about that."

The clerk is leaning back in his seat, almost at a diagonal against the window. Looks oddly luxuriant, but his breaths are coming shallowly and his voice is thin.

"Love is so hard," the clerk says. Wheezes.

Abe says, "Let's get outta here. Once we're on the road, I'll call the cops, and—"

"Wait. Before you start driving. Can you do me a huge favor?"

Something about the guy's demeanor has completely changed, and it's ringing all of Abe's alarm bells. But he doesn't know why. Nothing overtly threatening is happening. If anything, the guy seems almost. . . too relaxed.

"I've got asthma," the clerk says, chest rising in short little bursts. "It gets real bad sometimes. I can feel an attack coming on. Can you help me out?"

Abe feels a coldness creeping over his shoulders. Something is wrong. Something is very wrong. "What do you need?"

"Can you get my inhaler out of my backpack?"

The guy's backpack is sitting in the footwell. An unassuming black JanSport. Loose and floppy and seemingly empty.

"It's the only thing in there. You can't miss it."

"We really gotta go," Abe says. "We've wasted too much time already—"

"Please?" The clerk wheezes. *That's not an asthmatic wheeze, is it. . .?* "I could die if I don't have it. I'd do it but it hurts too much to bend. Because of the stab wounds. And if you're driving, then you can't get it either and—"

"Fine." If Abe had time to take that call from Jenna, he has time to do this. Fifteen seconds at most. Five, even.

But those alarm bells. . .

Abe reaches over and grabs the backpack. Unzips the top and sticks his hand in for the inhaler. There's a charging cord for a laptop but no—

White hot agony stabs into his hand and flares up his arm. He yelps, in surprise and pain. Wrenches his hand out of the bag.

No no no no.

Dangling from teeth sunk into the pinky-side of his palm is a thin snake. Alternating bands of black, yellow, and red. A black head.

And the clerk lets out another sigh.

And Abe realizes the quality of those shallow breaths.

Not asthmatic.

The clerk gives a satisfied, post-orgasmic moan. "Oh, *thank you.*"

OLD FRIENDS; FOREVER

Abe stares at the snake with clinical shock as it wriggles in mid-air, attached to his palm.

Then he looks back at the clerk.

The clerk is grinning the biggest grin Abe has ever seen. A grin that somehow adds decades to the clerk's boyish face—centuries—because only something truly ancient could feel a joy like this.

Abe's other hand is broken, of course. But now everything seems to be going numb, so he somehow manages to open the car door with his broken hand and throw himself backward onto the asphalt.

The snake finally lets go and slithers off into the night. Abe tries to do the same, backing away from the car, crawling across asphalt and concrete towards the safety of the convenience store.

Already, he's feeling sluggish.

Moving through molasses.

Nerves on fire.

Agonizing bursts sparking through him.

Concrete slabs drying around his limbs.

He's never moved so slow. Even the blood in his veins, turning into a hardened sludge.

The passenger side opens and the clerk slides out of the car.

"So," he says casually, like he just facilitated an introduction at a cocktail party, "that was a Sonoran coral snake. According to the sign on its case, it's super venomous, a neurotoxin, but not *always* fatal. It's pretty good at not overdoing it with its dosage when it bites as a warning. We'll see if she really meant business, I guess."

He sticks a hand into another compartment of his now-snakeless backpack and pulls out a slightly curved shield with an elastic strap. His mask.

Googly eyes are still stuck all over it, but fewer than before. All this action must be making the eyes come loose, fall off. It's apparent how homemade the thing is, this close to it.

There's something unusual about the surface of the mask too—something Abe might try to get a better look at to understand, but at the moment he's a little too preoccupied to care.

He reaches the front door to the store, somehow manages to pull himself up and inside, closes the door behind him. He looks for the locks on the door, sees one on the ground, tries to engage it but it's too complicated for his hands—one, broken, the other starting to inflate around its puncture marks. Plus, bending like this is making him feel even woozier.

The clerk saunters up to the door—too close, too late. He raps politely on the glass, his erratic smattering of eyes waggling.

Only one place to go.

One place Abe knows he can hide.

He gives up on locking the front door and stumbles across the snack displays until he reaches the bathroom.

This lock is much easier to engage. An old friend. He engages it as he hears the clerk skip his way through the convenience store, laughing.

Abe begins to laugh too.

No, cry.

No, laugh. Barely any energy to commit to either.

He slides down to the cold floor of the bathroom, joining the array of dead insects he'd left behind, and his eyes lose their focus. He stares towards the crack under the door, but really he's looking into the nowhere of nothingness.

"You're *such* a nice guy!" The clerk shouts from the other side of the metal. "It's seriously impressive! Like, you *really* try! Wow!"

Abe doesn't move.

"Honestly, though, it's good you didn't get on the road with me. Things were gonna get messy!"

Abe doesn't respond.

After a long, *long* silence, the clerk calls out again: "Just made it so your car won't start, FYI. We're stuck here together now. Maybe forever, I don't know."

Abe gives him nothing.

The room has been spinning ever so slightly, but whether it's the venom clogging his blood vessels or the stress of maybe losing his mind, he can't say. Doesn't matter. He kind of enjoys it. It's almost like being rocked to sleep.

SEVENTEEN

RECEIVING LINE; FINAL
GOODBYES; DEATH BEDS

"You were such a needy baby," his grandmother says from the broken glass on the wall and on the floor. "Oh, how you cried. I told your mother not to soothe you so often. It would only make you weak. I wasn't wrong."

He nods a little, perhaps in agreement, perhaps just as a concertgoer enjoying one of the hits.

"Sometimes I would look at you and wonder, is this it? Is this what we fled destruction for? I didn't like thinking this, believe it or not. You think me such a monster, but I don't *enjoy* this disappointment. It tastes horrible, Abraham. I simply wanted my grandchildren to remember where they came from. I wanted them to plant roots that couldn't be torn from the soil like mine were. Like my parents' were. My cousins'. Everyone we lost in the fire. I wanted my grandchildren to continue our traditions, because evil tried to take them from us, and what do we do in the face of evil? We do not say, 'Oh maybe you have a point, I'll keep it down, I'll put my faith and traditions away.' We spit in evil's eye and say, back to Hell with you, I come from a long line of survivors!

That's what it really is, boychik. I simply wanted you to survive. Every part of you."

"Welp," Abe mutters. "Sorry, Bobbe. Looks like that's not happening." His lips feel thick and dry. "Kein ayin hara, peh, peh, peh."

"*Quiet*," she snaps. "You didn't let me finish."

Wow. Can a mental projection get offended? He guesses so. Or maybe—he chuckles at this thought—maybe this conversation is *actually* happening. Maybe he and Bobbe, on their respective death beds, are in some shared, liminal, semi-conscious space?

Aw, good for us. Finally having something in common.

"I want to say. . . I was wrong about you," his grandmother says. He can hear the effort it takes to admit that. "You are a bad Jew. You never went to shul, you never honored Shabbos. But, Abraham, you are a *true* Jew. You have tried to endure."

"Didn't do a very good job of it, though, Bobbe."

"No, pupik," she agrees, kindly. "But that's not your fault. You know what I think? I think maybe the age you were born into, all these years of fat and comfort, this time between the great wars and whatever's coming next—and something *is* coming, you can feel it, can't you?—maybe this time has all just been some sort of. . . accident. An anomaly. Or a cruel joke. Or—"

"A rest stop," he mutters with a rueful laugh.

"*Yes*," she says around an appreciative smile. Then: "Are you familiar with the Buddha, Abraham?"

That question *really* takes him by surprise. He can't help but laugh. Like many other secular Jews he knows, he actually *has* dabbled a tiny bit in Buddhism. Something about that religion—its wisdom, its approach—always seemed particularly appealing to him. But to hear the word "Buddha" in his grandmother's voice? To hear her talk approvingly of any other culture? This either really *is* a conversation between two individuals, or his dying brain is throwing all sorts of ingredients at the wall while it struggles to stay online.

"I know, I know, I'm just an ignorant girl from a tiny village in Poland. You think I know nothing. But I have studied, too, Abraham. I have tried to make sense of this world. And a story sticks with me. A Buddhist teacher, with his students gathered around him—almost like a minyan, nu?—and he drinks out of a glass and says, 'I love this glass. It is so beautiful. It carries the water to my lips and keeps me alive. It catches the light. But if, one day, I accidentally drop it and it shatters, my heart breaks with it. I am so sad. So I must remember: being broken is the glass's truest nature. It will be broken far longer than it is whole. It is *meant* to be broken. It is *already* broken. How can I be sad then, for this brief illusion of wholeness?' Do you see what I'm saying, Abraham?"

Broken glass. That lesson he was searching for.

A strange feeling fills him. The opposite of snake venom.

"Thanks, Bobbe." He remembers the phrase she always ended conversations with, those rare occasions he spoke with her (was forced to speak with her) on the phone. "Zei gezunt and kim gezunt."

"You know what your problem is?"

His grandmother is gone. Now it's Ty's voice, coming from the mirror shards.

Oh great, is this a receiving line now?

"We don't have those in Jewish funerals," Abe mumbles.

Ty repeats: "You know what your problem is?"

Abe rolls his head on his neck, closes his eyes.

"I don't have any problems now. I'm ready to die."

"You know what your problem is?"

Maybe the fact that I've got a best friend who doesn't listen to me?

But no. This time it's not an imaginary conversation he's having. This time it's a memory. Ty *actually* said these words to him.

Okay, then. Bring on the memory.

One final moment before we turn off the lights and close up shop. No need for the whole worthless story to flash by. Make it a good one. Make it. . . *characteristic*.

Abraham Neer, this was your life.

EIGHTEEN

LIFE

"Abraham Neer, tonight, you're gonna be a fuck machine. You're gonna be the T-1000 of cum. They will turn your conquests into a billion-dollar film franchise. And you'll be awarded the Nobel goddamn Prize for your dong's breakthrough discoveries in perpetual motion."

With that, Ty handed Abe an overflowing fistful of condoms, each one a glaring neon. Abe recognized them from a previous club they'd played; offered for free in a fishbowl by the front door.

Abe looked at the collage of rubber in his palm. "Uh, what the fuck?"

The two of them were standing in the grimy bathroom of Club Congress. In thirty minutes, they were due to open a bill that had three other acts on it, but there was a decent crowd outside—mostly thanks to a nightly trivia event that had just finished up—and more than a few not unattractive women among it.

Not as many women as the over-generous amount of condoms Ty just shoved into his possession, though.

"'What the FUCK' is exactly right, my man! You're radiating pure sex tonight. You're shooting off pheromones like, like a skunk. But *good*. A s*ex skunk*."

Abe stared at his friend through narrowed eyes.

"Ty. What are you doing? This is gross."

"Not as gross as all the. . . y'know. . . all the sweet, sloppy poon you're about to get. Man. Ugh." That was too much, even for Ty. He grimaced at himself, the confident wingman disappearing. Ty, the concerned Scout Master, took over—a far more comfortable role. "Look. Dude. You need to get out there, okay? Get in the game. I never see you chatting with girls after shows. I mean," he dropped his voice to a conspiratorial low, "when was the last time you even—?"

"Jesus Christ."

"Whoa! The *Bible* days?"

Abe felt his face burning. He gave Ty a light, but not altogether unserious, shove.

"Would you stop? I'm not a casual hookup kinda guy, you know that."

"You're not an any-kind-of-hookup guy, I'm starting to think."

"Shut up. There's someone I've been kinda thinking about working my nerve up to ask out. It's fine. Don't worry about it."

Abe tried to hand the wad of condoms back and Ty said:

"Okay, but. . . what if that person isn't single anymore?"

Abe's stomach dropped. "What? What does that mean?"

"There's something I gotta talk to you about, man. It's. . . I've been wanting to tell you this for a couple weeks now and I don't know how. It's. . . a little awkward."

Abe somehow knew what Ty was about to say. He felt himself disassociate while Ty stumbled through a probably rehearsed speech about how he and Jenna had begun "hanging out" and were "maybe going to try being official about it." A parade of soft, equivocating language. A real vibe shift from the vulgar braggadocio a few minutes ago.

After an eternity, Ty finished. He looked at Abe for a response.

"Well." Abe swallowed a hot stone coated in dried shit. "That's all super. Happy for you."

He suddenly felt like this bathroom was too small for a single occupant, let alone two. He tried to leave, and Ty stopped him with a hand on his upper arm.

"Can we talk about this?"

"Talk about what? She's a person, not a PlayStation controller. She likes you. That's awesome. You're dumb and handsome, she's smart and beautiful, it's great. Good for the gene pool. Here."

He tried to hand the condoms back to Ty again—harder this time, practically punching Ty with them.

Again, Ty deflected the effort.

"We can't play a show with you pissed at me," he said.

"I'm not pissed at you."

"You're totally pissed at me."

And the thing was, Abe had never been more furious in his life. But it was a fury tinged with sadness. And it was a sadness tinged with fear. His heart was breaking at the prospect of losing this girl he'd developed overwhelming feelings for. But he also loved his friend and knew this was the sort of thing friendships ended over. He didn't want either to happen. But he also wasn't ready to swallow this indignity. Parts of him he never really thought about were suddenly flaring to life, reminding him of all the other indignities he'd swallowed in his life.

Suddenly, Ty's eyes lit up. "Do you want to hit me?"

"No, I don't want to hit you."

"Because you can. I'll allow it."

That made Abe laugh, a short, sharp snort. "What's the point of hitting someone if they allow it?"

"So you *do* want to hit me!"

"No! I want to get out of here and forget this fucking conversation."

This all seemed to be happening beyond him. Like he was watching a movie. He just wanted to be out of this bathroom, be among the crowds of people not there for him, drown his sorrow in a whiskey-ginger (*her favorite drink too; she got you into drinking them*), scream out his feelings onstage.

A cruel, condescending smile smeared across Ty's face.

"You know what your problem is?" he asked.

Abe's jaw clenched. "What? What's my problem?"

"You want things so badly, but I think *one* of the things you want is to never have to fight for the other things you want, and that makes it impossible to, y'know, have those other things! It's not even a vicious circle, man. It's a *stupid* circle."

"You saying *you* want to fight?"

"I mean, I'd *rather* not, but sometimes fighting's what you gotta do. Sometimes it's even kinda fun."

"Well, you're definitely making me want to fucking punch something! But I also don't want to hurt my hand before we go on, so! Fuck!"

The bathroom door pushed open. Some hapless schmuck, looking to piss. Abe and Ty shouted at him in unison to give them some space and he fled, eyes wide.

When they were alone again, Ty asked:

"So what do we do?"

"I don't want *these*, that's for fucking sure." Another attempt to be rid of the stupid goddamn condoms. Another rejection.

"Nope. Sorry. Not gonna let you. You might hate me, Abe, but I'm still your friend, and I'm looking out for your best interests. You're going to use those whether you like it or not."

"I'm not going to use them, Tyler. People don't like me like that."

"You're totally gonna use them! I'm gonna help!"

"I'M NOT GOING TO USE THEM."

"Abe!" Ty yelled. "Do you know I waited so long to actually ask Jenna out because I kept waiting to see if you'd do it first? Even *she* thought you were going to! And you never fucking did!"

Abe knew Ty was trying to goad him into attacking. That's not why Abe ultimately did. It wasn't anything Ty said—not even that last horrible, painful admission that would make Abe's heart hurt for the rest of its beats.

It was Ty's faint, smug grin. It made Abe think of someone else. Someone antagonistic and condescending who loved reminding him he was a failure. That he always feared the wrong monsters.

"Fine." Abe dumped the condoms onto the sink counter, began ripping their wrappers open. "You want me to use them? I'll fucking use them."

Ty looked on, curious.

Abe held the first condom under the faucet, filled it with water, and tied off the top. Then he did it again to a second.

He held two heavy water balloons in his hands and glared at Ty over a sneering smile.

"You wouldn't," Ty said. Suddenly nervous.

"Yeah, you're probably right," Abe agreed. Then threw the first balloon.

It exploded on impact against Ty's chest.

Ty yelped.

Abe threw the second one at Ty's shoulder.

"Look how fucking cheap these things are, asshole! Condoms shouldn't break like that!"

Ty didn't hear him; he was too busy mourning over his soaked outfit, too busy grabbing another condom and filling it up under the other sink. "You fucking *dick!*"

He was, of course, far more athletic than Abe, and his aim was unsurprisingly truer. He hit Abe square in the mouth with his balloon.

The fight immediately paused—a moment common in every boyfight; breath-holding combatants waiting to see how serious a potential injury might be, if the action needed to be halted or if things were about to get really nuts.

Then Abe growled, "I'm gonna fucking *murder* you," and the battle was on.

They got through almost half the condoms, turning the bathroom into a legitimately dangerous water hazard, before a bartender came in to see what the ruckus was.

Abe and Ty were summarily kicked out of Club Congress, their position on that night's bill revoked. They were told they'd never play there again.

Typical Ty, though: he managed to beg and plead with the club's booking manager for a second chance. He was just too charming and sincere to say no to. Another gig for Darwin's Foëtus was put on the club's calendar—but it was made clear, any shenanigans this time and they were gone for good.

Confirming that new gig was the last time Abe and Ty had spoken, until yesterday afternoon, when Abe informed Ty about his grandmother's stroke. In between, Ty had sent plenty of texts: pleas for rehearsal, for seeing a movie, for just grabbing a beer and hanging out. Abe ignored all of them. He was sure Ty would rather be hanging out with Jenna anyway.

Sometimes, though, he did wonder if Ty was right. Maybe Abe just needed to move on, play the field a little, stop putting so much emotional stock in someone who was now unavailable. Someone who was even more desirable now *because* of that unavailability. And someone whose unavailability was, in part, due to his own cowardice.

Maybe Abe should go to a bar, go to a concert, try to have a fling or two. He even stuck one of those damn neon condoms in his wallet, just to have it, just to look at it and remember that moving on *was* an option. The world didn't *have* to be so cruel. His heart might have been broken, but. . . well, it was like some Buddhist monk had said. Being broken wasn't cruelty, it was simply the state of things. At least he wasn't dead, right? Right. And while there's life, there's—

Abe's eyes open.

AFTERLIFE; ABE'S LAST CHANCE

He's not dead.

Somehow he isn't dead—at *all*.

In fact, he's actually feeling a tiny bit stronger. Still shaky and numb and a bit lightheaded, but sitting, resting, breathing, meditating, has helped.

Slowly, wobbly, he gets to his feet. Pulls out his wallet with thick, clumsy hands. That dumb, neon condom is still there. Glowing yellow, like an item in a video game.

He flexes the fingers of his bitten hand. They're swollen and stiff, but his thumb and forefinger are still relatively usable. Same with those fingers on his other, fractured hand. Two pincers, like a crab. Should be just enough to get the job done.

He bites open the wrapper, pulls out the thin prophylactic. Fills it with a little bit of water from the sink so it sags. Then he pumps some hand soap into it and resumes filling it with water.

Soon it's bulbous with soapy water. Enough to blind someone with a well-aimed shot in the face.

That lone googly eye on the bathroom tile catches his attention and he realizes he'll have to convince the guy to remove his mask. To hit him in his *real* eyes.

Can he even make a shot like that? Damaged as he is?

Abe leans his head against the bathroom door. This time he actually prays—*Baruch atah Adonai, Eloheinu melech ha'olam*...

That's all he remembers in Hebrew. The rest has got to come in English—but, hey, God speaks that, too, right?

Please help me get out of here.

Please, Adonai. Guide my hand. Help me survive.

Please. I don't want to break just yet.

He opens the bathroom door, the lock disengaging with a turn of the handle. For a moment, he worries the clerk might've locked him inside once more, but there's no resistance. The killer has been waiting for this final showdown. No need to prolong it anymore.

That said, once again the store appears empty.

Abe takes a step out of the bathroom, scanning for movement. Trying to summon every bit of action movie bravado he's ever seen or felt.

In this awful, straining silence, he gets the chance to really notice, dotted across the floor, the scores of random googly eyes that have been shed throughout the night. Like glitter after a party. Like rodent droppings. They all stare up at the ceiling. A final audience, at once avid and disinterested. Peripheral witnesses.

"If we're going to do this," Abe announces, "let's do this."

"Okay," a voice answers from the other side of the store. Muffled behind plastic. "Gimme a sec. I want you to tell me if something looks cool."

Abe tries to calm his galloping heart. Readjusts his hold on the soap grenade. He needs the bastard's eyes out in the open.

"Hey. How about no more masks, huh? Just you and me? Face to face?"

The clerk giggles.

"Come on," Abe pleads. "I've already seen you. You don't have to hide your face from me. *Please?*"

A long, considering pause.

"My face."

"It's only fair, right? Let me. . . appreciate the creator."

"Hm. Welllllllll, how about this?"

The clerk rises from where he was crouched behind a shelf.

He's not wearing a mask.

In fact, there's *nothing* above his neck.

He doesn't have a face at all.

Abe is so stunned by what he's seeing—by what he's *not* seeing—that the balloon squirms out of his grip and falls to the ground. It breaks open against the floor, spilling its contents uselessly, worthlessly across the tile.

Splat.

105

BROKEN; STAND-OFF; CHOREOGRAPHY; AN ANSWER AT LAST

Abe looks at the broken balloon at his feet. His grandmother might've commented on how inevitable this was.

She's silent, though. The whole world is silent.

Abe looks back up. Numb.

"Everything okay over there?" the clerk asks. "Did you drop something?" He cocks his neck, a pantomime of sympathy.

It's by that gesture that Abe understands what so startled him. The clerk *is* wearing a mask, after all—the same mask he's been wearing this whole time. But all of the eyes have finally been peeled off. What remains is a perfectly smooth, plastic-and-chrome mirror mask. Its flat surface reflects the store back at Abe and for that first moment, it had looked like there was no head at all.

The guy wouldn't have had any idea of Abe's plans, but it was still enough to make stupid, clumsy, shmendricky Abe drop his last, best hope. Dooming him.

"Doesn't matter," Abe says weakly.

"My face," the clerk says, "is *everything* now. Even your face! Do you see? Did it look cool?"

"Sure. Cool."

"Awesome. Okay!" The clerk holds up a knife. The biggest knife in the world. He waggles it, tantalizingly. "Still wanna 'do this?'"

Abe thinks about jumping back into the bathroom one more time. Locking the door. Coming up with some other plan. Maybe using the plastic scrub brush or one of the smaller shards of mirror glass.

He shakes his head at the idea. He's so tired. He won't forestall the inevitable anymore. He just wants to make it outside, at the very least. Be gutted in the fresh air.

He takes a small step away from the bathroom door.

The clerk responds with a hooting laugh and takes a big step toward Abe.

Abe might not have his balloon, but there's still plenty to throw. He picks up the nearest object off a shelf and launches it at the madman. Just a granola bar. It bounces harmlessly off the clerk's face. But it hit. His aim was true. So he grabs the next thing. And the next. And the next.

Chips. Pop tarts. Candy bars. Protein bars. He keeps a shelf in between them and throws everything he can. He only half-registers that he's emitting a hooting-laugh, too, the shadow twin of his pursuer's. A desperate, furious sound.

Gum. Bags of peppermint mints. Bags of circus peanuts. Bags of actual peanuts. All of them, hitting exactly where he's aiming.

Then, the door is behind him. It's *right there*.

Instead of throwing more snacks, he throws himself at the door. His hands actually close on the handle—

—but before he can get the door open, arms wrap around his midsection and hurl him backwards.

"No!" Abe shrieks, and receives a hooting cackle in response.

He was so close!

Could've been a knife in his back, he supposes. The same knife the clerk is waving in an uh-uh-uh motion right now. You're not leaving that easily, the gesture says.

A stand-off, then.

Abe tries to feint for the door, but the clerk matches his every move. Then the knife whips forward and slices Abe across the arm.

Abe seethes in pain, feels blood seep down his arm.

Worse, he's close enough that now he can see himself reflected back in that awful, chrome mask. He looks so small. So distorted. So helpless.

"No!" he shouts again, pleading.

"No!" the clerk mimics. "No! NononoNO!"

Abe looks around for other options. Run to the backroom? Run back around the store and try again for the front? Pretty much his only options, but—

While he's thinking, the clerk springs forward with the knife and cuts another deep wound in Abe's other arm before darting backwards. Abe snaps out of his thoughts; he's getting too groggy, too sloppy.

As if that realization was all the clerk was waiting for, the clerk springs forward again and this time Abe manages to avoid the slice by jumping backwards. His reflection shrinks in the mirror mask.

"There you go," the clerk says, approvingly. He lunges forward again—and Abe jumps backwards again.

And again. And again. Both of them moving in sync like expert line dancers. . . until Abe's feet forget the choreography. During his next dodge backwards, he tangles clumsily with himself and the next thing he knows, he's staring up at the ceiling, his back throbbing against the tile floor.

The clerk is on him in a flash. Sitting on his chest, trapping his arms.

"Oops!" The clerk laughs triumphantly, pityingly. Abe squirms underneath. Trapped.

The clerk is heavy. *Too* heavy. He must be putting his full weight on Abe's chest, but there's no way someone his size can be *so horribly* heavy.

"Why?" Abe manages, trying to breathe. "Why are you doing this?"

The clerk lets out another guffaw. "Why?! Haven't you figured this out yet?"

"No," Abe wheezes. "Figure out what? Please?"

"Don't you know what's happening? Don't you know who I am?"

"No! I don't know anything!"

The clerk bends his head towards Abe's. Stoops with impressive, maybe impossible, flexibility.

"Buddy," the clerk says. Calm. Rationally. "You've been calling my name all night." His breath, huffing delightedly against the inside of his mask. "Ask me."

"Who. . . are you?"

"I'm *God*," the clerk says. His voice fills the world.

Abe stares back at his own terrified face and realizes the man isn't kidding.

GOD VERSUS ABRAHAM;
THE RED SEA;
NILS LOFGREN; COMPANY

So heavy. So unbearably heavy.

"What?" Abe asks dumbly.

The clerk gives another hardy laugh. "*You're* my creation. All of this is my creation. But I get *soooo* bored sometimes, so I come down to visit. To keep from going crazy."

"You *are* crazy."

"Ha! Yeah, well."

"You're not God, you're, you're—"

"*Everything.* Look at me."

The mask presses against Abe's nose. And maybe it's because it's so hard to breathe, or maybe it's the lingering effects of the snake venom, but Abe looks into his own terrified, bewildered eyes, sees the swirling prism of the reflective surface, and begins to understand. Yes. Yes, this may very well be so, his attacker may indeed be telling the truth. This man. This stranger. This crushing weight on his chest, dense as a dying star. This *is* God. *The* God. The one countless generations of terrified humans once worshipped. The one countless more generations try to pretend they *aren't* worshipping now.

The God of lightning in the desert. The God of twisted shadows on cave walls. The God of wrath. Of persecution. Of corruption. The God that demands proper nouns and capitalization. The God whose first commandment isn't kindness or empathy, but THOU SHALT HAVE NO OTHER GOD BEFORE ME. The God of sick jokes. The God of babies born without heads. The God of turtles born having to race to the sea with their first lungful of air. The God of ancient land disputes that turn into genocidal rugby matches. The God of the great cosmic punchline that is mortality foreknown. Of suns destined to implode. Of nerve endings that refuse to stop reporting pain. Of fathers who die of bowel cancer. Of hearts that won't stop breaking. Of promising futures and the unbearably slow deflation from pinprick disappointments.

"I can do whatever I want," the clerk—God—is crowing. "You're my creation! And I just wanna drink you up!"

Abe stares at his own face, braces himself for God to bring His knife down into Abe's fragile, mortal chest. Splinter his ribs, pop his lungs and heart, spray his chin with hot blood.

God doesn't do that, though. Instead, He starts casting around for something new. Something fun. He lands on an item displayed on one of the racks nearest them. "Ooo!" He reaches out and grabs it. A glint of light flashes before Abe's eyes. Something metal.

"Drink! You! Up!" God exclaims again, waggling the metal object in front of Abe. It takes a moment to focus on what it is: a souvenir bottle opener. The kind with a round mouth that encircles a bottle cap . . . and a sharp under-tooth that pops the cap off.

God sets the bottle opener on Abe's face and gets to work.

"Pop top!" God proclaims in delight. "Chug-a-lug!"

Abe feels the chill of the metal, then a digging. A scraping.

The sharp under-tooth bites into Abe's nose, his septum, his upper lip. The pain is exquisite. Symphonic. Multipart. Polyrhythmic. Deliciously complex. It's prog-pain.

The shredding of layer upon layer of skin. The cold, bitter metal, and hot, bitter blood. The uncompromising squeeze of the round bottle opener around the bulb of his nose. The frantic furrowing as God works the metal over and around and into his skin, like an overzealous dentist with horrible depth perception. The sounds of teeth and flesh being scraped.

The under-tooth chews into Abe's septum, up and down, up and down, back and forth, until, with a luxuriant rip, the septum separates from the cleft of Abe's upper lip. The flesh at the bottom of Abe's nose puckers backwards like a shirt bunched up against a chair, like blankets kicked to the foot of a bed, revealing a deepening hole, a third nostril in his philtrum where the bottle opener continues to dig.

Abe's mouth floods with blood.

My nose, he thinks dimly. *I always thought it got in the way.*

He's going to peel my face off.

God's going to peel my face off and I'm going to drown in my own red sea.

Nothing I can do about it. It's Moses who parts the sea. It's Jacob who wrestles and wins. All I can do is—

An unexpected image flashes in his memory. Nils Lofgren, executing somersaults while shredding lead lines during an E-Street Band concert. Years ago, Abe had watched video of those moves and, ever since, had been desperate to try something similar onstage. He'd never played venues big enough to try, and was always afraid of getting tangled in cords, but none of that is an issue here.

—all I can do is roll with it.

God is leaning forward in His exertion. The weight is off of Abe's arms and chest a little. Abe scooches his feet and legs further up and, with a final burst of strength, pushes up. He somersaults backwards, taking God with him, flipping and scattering them both across the floor.

Abe staggers to his feet, the front of his face a copper-flavored waterfall. All the blood he can't swallow drools down his chin. Distantly, he feels the loose flesh under his nose trying to settle back into place.

Meanwhile, splayed out in front of him, God's mask has slipped off His face a little. He appears confused about what just happened. . . then His mouth brightens with a delighted smile. He rises, in no hurry. Adjusts His mirror mask so it's back in place.

Abe's move got him out from being trapped, but their relation to the door hasn't changed—God still stands between Abe and freedom.

Abe looks around for an escape route. Realizes, once again, his options haven't changed. Fine. Let him die amongst the bugs.

In a limping, clumsy run, Abe doubles back to the bathroom, his wet gasps of exertion barely audible under God's appreciative laughter and the tacky squelch of their shoes against the drying blood on the floor.

God follows, close behind, swiping the knife, easily closing the distance. Managing to get a few more knicks and slices in before Abe reaches the bathroom doorway.

Abe sees the puddle of soapy water a split second before his body takes control and leaps over the spill. His jump takes him face-first into the bathroom wall, but he stops himself with his palms and turns around just in time to see God, not so lucky, slip and literally fly up into the air before crashing down onto His back.

The crack of God's head against the floor makes Abe's teeth hurt.

God groans and twitches like an upturned turtle. As painful as the fall appears to have been, though, He won't be incapacitated for long. Already He's trying to get up on His elbows.

Abe doesn't think he can step over and sprint to the door fast enough, so he hustles to the bathroom and, straddling the draped body of the rattlesnake, lifts up the lid of the toilet tank.

It's heavier than he's expecting. Hard to hold, especially given his injured hands. But he brings it back over to the clerk and holds it high.

One of God's hands wraps around Abe's ankle. Abe reacts without thinking and, instead of bringing the lid down on God's head, he drops it on the arm holding onto his leg. The hand lets go and Abe is able to stumble backwards, losing his balance and landing on his butt back in the bathroom.

Looks like he broke God's wrist, though. The fingers of the affected hand are twitching and pointing in uncomfortable looking directions. God seethes in pain, in the effort of sitting up, spittle audibly spraying against the inside of the mask.

"Oh wow," God keeps saying in a monotone. "Oh wow. Oh wowwwww. Wow, wow, wow."

The porcelain lid has broken into shards. God picks one of them up with His good hand and starts crawling on His knees and elbows towards Abe. The shard is jagged and brutal looking. A raptor claw.

"Wow. Wowee wow, wow. Wowowowowowowow."

Abe sees his own twisted fury and surprise as the mask approaches. The lower half of his face, mangled and ruined, drenched in a beard of blood and gore.

God advances on all fours. An animal on the hunt. One merciless, porcelain claw tapping on the ground. He's obviously hurt and dazed, His breath is ragged. But He's also not stopping.

Abe retreats in a reverse crabwalk, over insect carcasses, further into the bathroom until the cold, hard wall stops him.

He can't move backwards any further, only to the side.

God gets closer. Closer.

"Wait," Abe says in a breathy whisper. He has to spit blood out of his mouth to not accidentally aspirate on it. "Wait, please."

That changes God's droning wows to waits: "Wait, wait, wait, wait. Waitwaitwaitwaitwait."

Abe is in the corner now. Nowhere to go.

"Just one second," Abe gasps. "I just have to tell you something. It's important."

His own desperate expression, reflected back at him.

"What is it, little one?" God asks.

Abe swallows. It takes great effort. He has no idea what's going to come out of his mouth next. Only that he must fascinate his assailant.

"I love you," he blurts.

The clerk's head tilts. "What?"

"I *love* you," Abe says again. Staring at himself. "I'm so grateful for all you've done. All you've given me. Thank you for. . . for music, for sunsets, for laughter, for sex, for, for, for Icees and beef jerky and satisfying pees. Thank you for life! Thank you for so much life! I love you!"

God takes this in. Sits back on His haunches.

"You. . . l—? No you don't."

"With all my heart. With all my mind. With all my strength. I absolutely fucking *love* you." Puts all the sincerity he can into those three words.

God's shoulders twitch. Then He begins to laugh. Great, belly laughs. He pushes the reflective mask off of His young/

ancient face to reveal delighted tears streaming down His cheeks. He keeps trying to speak and each time, another gale of laughter overtakes Him.

"That's—! That's the stupi—!"

Abe knew he might get a reaction, but the extent of this reaction is a surprise.

No matter. He takes his opportunity. Quicker than he would've thought possible, he reaches for the one thing in grabbing distance: the midsection of the dead rattlesnake. He yanks the snake from out under the toilet lids and whips it forward.

He misses God's face. It lands somewhere even better.

The head of the snake collides straight on with God's neck. And even though it should be impossible, even though it defies every odd, the snake's posthumous bite reflex proves true.

Its teeth latch onto the Creator of the universe's throat.

Right into His carotid and jugular. Right next to His ridiculously-named Adam's apple.

God's eyes go wide with almost comical surprise.

Abe's own eyes do the same.

On this day, a miracle occurs, he thinks, and lets go of the snake.

God stumbles backwards, trying to laugh, trying to whoop, trying to pry the snake from His neck, trying to get to His feet. He finally manages to pull the dead snake off, but then He slips again in the soap puddle and flails backwards, making a real farcical performance of crashing into the nearest display of snacks.

In His flailing, one of the thin hangers holding snacks gets jammed into one of His eyes. It goes in deep. He begins to seize, blood transubstantiating into jellied cranberry sauce. He knocks snacks everywhere. Makes horrible choking noises. Spasming. Foaming. Twitching. His bowels let go. Piss darkens His pants.

It's an agonizing scene.

Abe takes no pleasure in it.

He simply watches from where he's slumped against the bathroom wall, enjoying the cool solidity of the tile and the quiet that eventually comes.

XXX

He sits that way for a long time.

Eventually, the outside world lights up with blues and reds. Is it real this time? He thinks so. But what's the difference? He's still enjoying the wall, its calmness, its simplicity. So much elegance in a wall. What a blessing to simply hold up a ceiling. What a creation.

His eyes never leave the clerk's face. The guy wasn't God after all, was he? Just some normal, damaged human being? And this was nothing more than an unfortunate encounter in an isolated gas station convenience store in the middle of the night?

Abe just keeps staring at that young, innocent face. His eyes—one glazed and half-lidded in death, the other skewered and leaking. What stars imploded within those eyes? What universes were wiped out?

The first cop who finds Abe actually screams. Not just because Abe looks like pure hell, but because he's sitting there, practically carpeted in bugs.

A whole array has found him, trailing down from the vent and from a missing panel in the ceiling. Another box's cargo. Spiders. Centipedes. Taking their time to investigate what's happening below.

Abe doesn't show them any mind.

In fact, he feels blessed by their gentle company.

A MAN IN GOD'S IMAGE
A GOD IN MAN'S IMAGE

They found the van around the corner from the crime scene. Parked on the shoulder of the road. The clerk (who, of course, wasn't actually a clerk, just someone wearing clothes stolen from one of the dead employees) had moved it, presumably to aid in his fucking with Abe. Saving it for some big reveal. Perhaps if Abe had got on the road more expediently—if Jenna hadn't called—the clerk was going to point the van out before dumping the snake in his lap or something. No way to know. Things played out the way they'd played out.

It takes almost a year and a half of bureaucratic wrangling before Abe is able to buy the van from the police department.

He imagines they might be confused as to why he'd want it. Or maybe they're not. He doesn't really care. They take his cash easily enough.

Besides. Forensics cleaned it out thoroughly. There are no clues inside for him to find. It's just a van now.

He doesn't need any clues. He's not interested in learning more. He just . . . wants it.

First thing he does is give it a new license plate. Some random letters and numbers. No message. Something like a cramp inside his heart eases up a little when he does that.

Funny how the driver's seat feels like cold tile, though.

In fact, he *always* feels cold tile on his back.

And sometimes his vision seems just ever-so-slightly framed by tile walls.

Like he's looking at the world through a bathroom doorway.

XXX

Jenna and Ty are still going strong—they really *do* make sense as a couple, and Abe actually enjoys the dynamic of the three of them, whenever they're together.

It's not jealousy that keeps him from hanging out with them more often. It's a stranger reason than that; one he finds hard to articulate.

He doesn't always recognize them anymore.

He'll be having a good enough time, but suddenly he'll wonder, *Who are these people?*

Who am I around them?

What are we doing here?

What are we all becoming?

What have we become?

Then he'll think:

We're all just biding our time before we break, aren't we?

This is just the rest stop.

He's happy they're happy. He's happy happiness exists. Even if it's only for now.

But usually, he's much more comfortable alone, sitting against the cool tile, wherever he happens to be.

He doesn't know how much longer Darwin's Foëtus will stay together. He knows Ty wants to play out more—in part because he thinks it's good for Abe's healing process, and in part because the band has never sounded better.

The few gigs they've played have been marvelous. Abe's playing is impeccable. Even when he misses a note, it sounds incredible. And his singing has improved. All that screaming seems to have made his voice richer, deeper. The emotion he puts into the lyrics often leaves audience members in tears.

Abe never met his grandfather—Bobbe Meydl's husband, who died well before Abe was born—but his mom told him he was a cantor. He had the most beautiful singing voice, she'd say. He put all his pain and hurt into it.

In the middle of songs, Abe's able to forget everything. But he's not sure it's worth it. The way everything comes flooding back afterwards, it's like being bitten by some venomous creature—he knows it won't kill him, but he has to feel his blood congeal all over again.

xXx

The most effective way he's found to clear his mind is driving around in his van. When he's behind the wheel, all that matters is what's in front of him. And, of course, the cool tile against his back.

Sometimes it's just aimless driving.

Sometimes he makes the long trip out to visit Bobbe.

She's in a nursing facility now. Still holding on, two years later. Making the tiniest bit of improvement too. A wiggled finger. A blink.

He overhears one of her doctors say, *Honestly, I think she's too stubborn to die.*

Abe thinks, *Thank God for that. Baruch Hashem.*

He thinks, *L'dor, v'dor.* Generation to generation. Doorway to doorway.

He thinks, *Tikkun olam.* Of repairing the world.

He doesn't speak when he visits. He doesn't hold her hand. He doesn't feel that kind of sentimentality about her. He just sits by her side. Maybe that'll change one day—he feels like they have a lot to talk about. He wonders if she can relate to the strange thoughts and fantasies he's had lately. He suspects she can.

In the meantime, he's content to share space with her.

The bathroom walls feel very tight around him when he's there in the hospital, though.

He's still not sure if that's a good or a bad thing.

xXx

He bears a lot of physical scars from his night at the gas station. Most extreme, of course, was from the damage incurred by the bottle opener. But with a few stitches and a little bit of time, mostly all that remains are a few thin lines bisecting his philtrum and upper lip.

In a way, it almost looks like the surgical remnants of a harelip.

He stares at it in the mirror a lot. It actually looks great. Dignified. Mysterious.

It does make him think strange thoughts, though.

I'm the Hairlip Man now.

He often wonders. . . could I ever be like my grandmother's boogeyman? Do I have that kind of evil—that kind of *h8*—in me?

He wonders, did that man *also* think of himself as God? Is that what it takes to be so cruel?

Abe remembers his own twisted, bloody image, reflected back at himself.

What kind of God would I be?

What kind of universe would I create?

Often when Abe goes driving, he starts before dawn. He likes to be in the van to watch the sun come up, then drive slowly around in the soft, pale light, when the backroads are empty, and he can take his time.

He encounters a lot of joggers on these drives.

Eager early birds, getting their exercises in before another day of blissful productivity.

He's fascinated by them. Stares at them from behind the wheel of his great big van.

Sometimes he's filled with such a rage it almost takes his breath away. They have it so *easy*. They're so fucking ignorant of what life can be like.

He's started to have incredibly vivid fantasies. The kind that are so real they make him wonder if he really just *did it*.

Running them down.

Hearing surprised yelps and the chicken-bone snaps of their skeletons under his weight. Feeling the tires jump and twitch over their bodies.

Crunch.

Splat.

Sometimes he wonders if he should try it. Just once.

It would be so easy to nudge the steering wheel a little to the side, press a little harder on the gas.

He can imagine how easily the van would sail over their bodies, grind them into the asphalt of the shoulder.

He can imagine how the springs would compensate. How he would rock and bounce in his tile-wall seat behind the wheel.

Maybe, if he did it enough times, it would be enough to finally rock him out of place.

Maybe he'd be shaken free from his bathroom.

Some mornings, he thinks he could run down four or five people before the authorities even notice.

Is this the feeling of being broken? He wonders. *Or is it the process of breaking?*

Is this how it feels to refuse to break?

Or is every moment simply its own act of creation? Its own god, too holy for a name?

He doesn't know.

He always keeps the wheels on the road and pointed forward, though.

Steady as can be.

ACKNOWLEDGMENTS

Thank you to Alan, you Shortwave genius. You do such amazing work and I'm honored by your dedication to this release. (But please go get some rest, okay?)

Thank you to Tor Nightfire, beautiful and beloved home of my full-length work, for allowing me this side-adventure.

Thank you to Nancy LaFever and Erin Foster.

Thank you to my agent, Alec.

Thank you to my wife, Kelley.

Thank you to my Table of Discontents.

Thank you to everyone who was excited when this novella was announced and made me feel like maybe we weren't crazy for putting it out. As a semi-retired indie theatermaker, I'll always have a deep love for the indie scene—that's where the truly wild stuff happens—and a sincere appreciation for all who support it. (Of course, thanks for also supporting the trad presses, too, where you can preorder my next full-length, plug plug plug.)

Most of all, thank *you*, dear reader. I wrote almost all of the first draft of this in between *Mary* and *Nestlings* and, if you're a fan of either, I hope you find it kinda neat how there are little echoes of each in this story. Writing sometimes feels like unclogging a sink—often, after it's finally all drained out, there's still a little residue left over. On that romantic note...

Rest Stop is entirely fictional, except for one detail: the existence of that van with the particularly ominous license plate. I crossed paths with it once, many, many years ago, and count myself lucky it was a fleeting encounter. I hope that's the last I ever see of it, and I hope it never finds you, either.

Speaking of hopes...

I hope you'll consider donating to Doctors Without Borders or World Central Kitchen or any other organizations dedicated to protecting lives during humanitarian crises. This story is, in part, about the emotional scars inflicted by historical trauma, and, as of this writing, there are currently some very, very contemporary traumas being wrought upon innocent people. To go into a deeper discussion here (as I attempted in previous drafts) kinda hijacks the book in its very final pages, which isn't fair to anyone—but given that this *is* the Acknowledgments page, I wanted to at least acknowledge that.

Lastly, and not unrelatedly, if you're reading this when it's originally published, we're just a couple weeks away from the 2024 US Presidential Election. Go inform yourself on the issues you care about, volunteer, send some postcards, knock on some doors, and most of all, please, please, *please*, make sure you vote. It really does matter who's behind the wheel—and cynicism and disengagement only help the darkest forces into the driver's seat.

Until the next one,
NAT CASSIDY
New York, May 2024

NAT CASSIDY writes horror for the pages, stage, and screen. He's the author of the acclaimed novels *Mary: An Awakening of Terror* and *Nestlings*. His books have been featured in best-of lists from Esquire, Harper's Bazaar, NPR, the Chicago Review of Books, the NY Public Library, and more, and he was named one of the "writers shaping horror's next golden age" by Esquire.

natcassidy.com

A NOTE FROM SHORTWAVE

Thank you for reading *Rest Stop*! If you enjoyed this novella, please consider writing a review. Reviews help readers find more titles they may enjoy, and that helps us continue to publish titles like this.

For more Shortwave titles, visit us online. . .

OUR WEBSITE
shortwavepublishing.com

SOCIAL MEDIA
@ShortwaveBooks

EMAIL US
contact@shortwavepublishing.com

The businessman and the doctor sit in the doctor's private office deep in the bowels of the massive new medical complex.

"Holeeeeeeeeeee shit," the businessman says. He's barely in his forties, but comfort and success have kept the years from his face, making him look more like the homecoming king he once was than the adult he currently is. But there's an edge in his eyes all the same. Broken glass behind the poster boy perfection that no amount of money can sweep up. He's sitting in a leather chair facing the doctor's shining, cherry oak desk. "Wow, wow, wow."

This is not a medical examination. This is not a room for such things. This is a room for meetings, for dealings.

It's a room for business.

The doctor blushes and raises a rocks glass half-filled (or half-empty, depending on your view of things) with amber liquor worth more than the monthly income of the average American.

"The exciting world of hospital administration!" she exclaims. She's older. Well put together, but her pampering has come later in life, after hard-fought battles, tough decisions, bare-knuckle brawls, and, of course, so much downward pressure.

The businessman meets her toast with his own similarly half-filled—or half-empty–glass.

"And how many doctors under you now?"

"Seven trauma teams, six of the world's top plastic surgeons, and more specialists than we can afford. Plus the psych ward which takes up most of the east wing."

"Look at you," the businessman says. "If I had a hat—" He makes a doffing gesture.

"Aw, you should buy yourself a hat! Life is short! Use those whiz kid tech bucks for something fun."

"Yeah. Right. . ."

A cloud crosses the businessman's face and for the first time the doctor notices how deep-set his eyes have become.

"Uh-oh." The doctor's brow furrows. "Looks like you have something to say."

He shrugs. "I've always got something to say."

"Is it about why you wanted to see me?"

"I mean, I wanted to see my favorite doc in her fancy new digs, but. . ." He stares into his glass. "Are you okay to, um, talk shop a little?"

"Harris. Do I really need to remind you about how your patronage changed my life? I wouldn't be in these new digs without you. For you, I'm always okay to 'Talk. Shop.'"

Her lips form enticing shapes. Her plosives pop and snap. But he isn't enticed. He seems troubled. Shaken.

"Doctor/patient?" he asks.

"Doctor/patient."

He swallows another mouthful of luxurious, silken liquor.

"I think I'm going crazy." Then he corrects himself. "Gone. I think I've gone crazy."

The doctor leans forward. She is a friend, but she is also a doctor.

"I'm listening."

The businessman takes a deep breath and tells her.

"So. . . a couple weeks ago. . ."

XXX

Harris sat at his marble counter top. He was eating cereal—cereal was mostly all he was up for eating these days. He'd never been one for cooking, and now? The kitchen was too big. A foreign country where he didn't speak the language.

He hadn't shaved or showered in quite some time either.

He was in a daze—so much so that he didn't even jump when his wife, Emily, came into the room.

She moved with some speed.

"Don't forget," she said, going through the gestures of her Running Out the Door ritual, "your suit needs to be picked up. And we need a refill for the seltzer thingy. I love you more than bunches."

She kissed him on the head and a few seconds later the front door closed behind her.

Harris sat frozen, halfway through bringing a spoonful of cereal to his lips.

There was no noise for a very long time until the spoon dropped from his numb fingers and crashed loudly into the bowl.

XXX

The doctor stares at the businessman. She doesn't want to admit that she doesn't understand, so she runs what he said back again in her mind several times. She comes up with nothing.

"Harris," she says at last. "Here's where you tell me what I'm—" She's going to say *missing*, but before that word can emerge, the businessman says:

"My wife died six months ago. Car crash."

"Oh." The doctor's mouth dries up in a flash.

"Yeah."

"Harris, I'm so... How did I not...?"

He waves a dismissive hand. "Please. We haven't seen each other in... We've both been busy." He takes another sip. "Anyway. The things she said? About my suit and the seltzer thingy? Those were the last things she said to me the day she died. She got into one of her cars and... and later that night there was an accident. A bad one. Couldn't even identify the body visually; they had to use her dental..." Saying it all out loud overwhelms him for a moment. He quickly shakes it off. Clears his throat, finishes his drink. The doctor seamlessly provides a refill.

He continues. "But I know what you're thinking. To people of our, heh, economic vantage point, spouses are usually the obstacle. Right? It's like most rich assholes stay married just to have someone to scheme around. Not me. I *loved* her. I loved her so damn much. And I know it wasn't the easiest marriage, she had to put up with a lot. My working all the time. And my temper. I knew she wasn't always happy. Hell, I'm pretty sure she was going to leave me sooner or later. But I would have done anything to keep her. She... she was the apogee."

"Good word," the doctor says, her heart breaking for her friend.

"Yeah. And then I lost her anyway." He's back to staring into his drink again.

"Wait, but you said this thing in the kitchen... with your wife... was a couple weeks ago. How—if she died six months ago—?"

His eyes meet hers–sparkling with, what, sarcasm? Dark humor? Mania?

"Weird, right? The next morning, I thought maybe I'd imagined it, you know? I mean, I had *just* reached that stage of grief where the waters were ebbing a little. It's like you're buried up to your neck in sand with the tide crashing in on you, but it'd finally started to recede, I could grab a gulp of air and maybe—"

XXX

"Don't forget," his dead wife said again, "your suit needs to be picked up. And we need a refill for the seltzer thingy. I love you more than bunches."

Harris was back at his marble counter top. He'd poured himself an identical bowl of cereal. He was wearing the same set of dirty pajamas. The only difference was this time he was shaking too badly with anticipation to hold a spoon. He'd been waiting to see if she'd show up.

When she kissed him on the head he jumped as if electrocuted. She giggled and continued for the door.

"What are you doing?" He heard himself asking. "Emily? Are you—?"

She giggled again and, with an all-too-familiar slam, the door closed and she was gone.

It took Harris a few moments to find his legs again. He ran out the door, but. . . nothing. No sign of her (other than all the signs he hadn't yet removed in his newfound position as widower).

Until the next morning, when she came back again at the exact same time.

"Don't forget your suit needs to be picked up. And we need a refill for the seltzer thingy. I love you more than bunches."

She kissed him on the head and disappeared.

And then the next morning.

"Don't forget your suit needs to be picked up. And we need a refill for the seltzer thingy. I love you more than bunches."

She kissed him on the head and disappeared.

And the next morning.

And the next morning.

And—

XXX

"And you get it," the businessman tells the doctor.

She's aghast. "How long did this go on?"

"About five or six days before I couldn't go downstairs anymore. I got too unnerved, so I started hiding upstairs to avoid her." He swallows. The doctor can hear his throat click even from where she's sitting. "And that's when the voicemails started."

"Harris." The doctor puts a hand flat on her desk, effectively pressing pause on the proceedings. "Do you want me to get a team of paranormal investigators together? I have contacts that are, I mean, they're as reputable as they *can* be in that field, but—"

"Just listen." He gets up and pours himself another drink. He tops off the doctor's as well. A sly smile has crossed his lips. "I'm not even close to done..."

TO READ MORE, BUY THE
CHAPBOOK SERIES AVAILABLE
EXCLUSIVELY FROM
SHORTWAVE PUBLISHING

FROM THE CASSIDY CATACOMBS

AVAILABLE NOW!

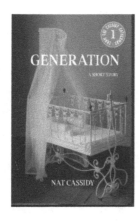

ALSO AVAILABLE FROM SHORTWAVE PUBLISHING

ALSO AVAILABLE FROM SHORTWAVE PUBLISHING

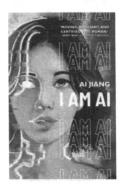

ALSO AVAILABLE FROM SHORTWAVE PUBLISHING

ALSO AVAILABLE FROM SHORTWAVE PUBLISHING

ALSO AVAILABLE FROM SHORTWAVE PUBLISHING

Printed in the USA
CPSIA information can be obtained
at www.ICGtesting.com
CBHW011145111024
15703CB00022B/1943

9 781959 565369